pseud. "Two friends"

Panjabi Sketches

pseud. "Two friends"

Panjabi Sketches

ISBN/EAN: 9783337013684

Printed in Europe, USA, Canada, Australia, Japan

Cover: Foto ©Andreas Hilbeck / pixelio.de

More available books at **www.hansebooks.com**

PANJABI SKETCHES

BY TWO FRIENDS

INTRODUCTION BY

SIR WILLIAM MUIR, K.C.S.I.

LL.D., D.C.L., PH.D. (*Bologna*)

WITH EIGHT ILLUSTRATIONS

London: Marshall Brothers

Paternoster Row E C

C.E.Z.M.S. 27 Chancery Lane W C

1899

LIST OF ILLUSTRATIONS

INTRODUCTION

I VERY gladly respond to the call of the C.E.Z.M.S. for an Introduction to this charming little work. The anonymous authorship of *Punjâbi Sketches* is double; namely, by a Lady and a Gentleman both well known to me. The latter, having been long in the Punjab, is well acquainted both with Official and Missionary work there, and hence is able admirably to describe, as here, the outward surroundings and business habits of the people. The other contributor laboured for many years in the same Province as a Missionary of the C.E.Z.M.S., and is therefore thoroughly qualified to give us an insight into Zenana life.

The story, interesting in itself, affords a close and living picture of the family life and everyday habits of our Indian peasantry, Hindoo, Sikh, and Moslem. Still more, it illustrates the influence of Missionary work, and the harvest springing up every here and there from the good seed scattered at the hands of our Zenana ladies. And yet even more telling, it brings to light the terrible difficulties of the convert cast forth from his home with bitter indignation by all around, and severed, possibly for ever, from all that has hitherto been to him most dear and precious.

Gazing thus on scenes told by our anonymous friends with such life and vigour, the reader will hardly be surprised to hear that another well-known work, *Not by Might*,[1] is

---

[1] *Not by Might.* Office of C.E.Z.M.S., 27, Chancery Lane, W.C.

by the same hand that has contributed her share of the present *Sketches*. In that charming and prettily illustrated little volume, besides a well-drawn picture of village life with all its Hindoo surroundings, we have also a faithful exhibition of the Moslem faith, and of its bigotry and persecuting zeal. This most attractive work, though it has already reached a second edition, is not so widely known as it might be. Powerfully adapted to stir up our interest in Indian homes, it deserves, and will I hope obtain, a much wider circulation than it has yet received amongst the supporters of the various Zenana Societies throughout the land.

And yet there is a third little Tractate, no less powerful and attractive, by the same hand, viz., *Seed Time and Harvest; a Tale of the Punjab*, by A. D. It was printed in India in 1898, by the CHRISTIAN LITERATURE SOCIETY. The books of that Institution are for use in India only, and not sent to this country. A copy, however, of this little work happening to fall into our hands, the Christian Literature Society were so impressed with its value, as bringing the claims and virtue of Zenana evangelization before our people at home, that a large edition is being published in this country, where it deserves to be even better known than in India.

The scene is Lahore, which is described with such grace and energy that the City with its lanes and buildings, the country and its villages surrounding, are pictured as if all lay before your very eye. The Hindoo family life is described with graphic brightness. The story runs that Narain Dās is converted along with his widowed sister; she falls sick, and her burial forces him to confess the truth, hitherto hidden from his parents, who repulse him with scathing indignation. Expelled by them, he finds work in the City in company with English and Native friends. At last he is attacked and dangerously wounded by a mob stirred up by an angry relative, and obliged to follow his profession in other Provinces. After some years his father falls sick, and his illness leads to his conversion, recall of his son, and restoration of the whole family. It is all told with a pathos which at times might well bring a tear to the eye, and with a power that unconsciously draws the heart along with it. This tiny Tractate of but threescore pages, places well before us the Hindoo home and its surroundings; the call for Missionary and Zenana work; and the possibilities, through it, of the higher life beyond. May the little jewel be blessed to many and incline their hearts to help forward the great work in India.

A. D.'s only fault is that she sometimes drops an ideal character just at the point when we want to follow it to the happy end. Thus the charming Chand Kor is left standing beside her frenzied father and embittered mother, and we hear no more of her. Will A. D. not follow our friend back to her husband at Amritsar, and tell us of her future life? And so also with Kishen Dei, and her gallant son's experience in the African corps; and "of the light arisen at eventide to the old folks at home."

One cannot too highly congratulate a Society which is able to send forth such labourers as the Writer of these little books, nor fail earnestly to wish them God-speed wherever in India or elsewhere in the Missionary field they plant their footsteps.

W. MUIR.

EDINBURGH,
May, 1899.

CHAPTER I

THE village of Maure lay flat and still at the dawn, for within its mud walls all living things were asleep. Not a breath stirred the leaves of the pipal tree at the gate, nor touched the calm surface of the little stream—a tributary of one of the five great rivers of the Panjab—which crept along in the slow, hesitating manner of its uncertain and winding course.

It was quiet and peaceful as a child asleep. But the stillness was not of long duration; for in that great hot plain, where it seems always noontide, night yields without delay to morning.

The sky quickened, and ere long the sun, with all the power of the month of May, rose like the strong man rejoicing to run a race, and the cup of the world was soon filled to the brim with golden light. It poured over the village walls, chasing the blue shadows back towards the inner rooms, filtered through crevices, pierced the overlapping leaves of the pipal with pungent points of fire, and opened the eyes of the last and laziest sleeper with its burning touch. The village therefore which but a short time ago looked like a child asleep was now, in the same manner, vastly like a child awake—the child which awakes with a cry—and so it began a new day.

Perhaps the last to wake up were the inmates of the largest house in the place, a house whose stuccoed front of white faced the narrow street. The white wall aforesaid was adorned with pictures of two wrathful figures in red, standing

11

beside two palm trees in green, and above sat a benign-looking
man, smiling affectionately in the direction of a group of blue
stars. A row of peacocks, also in stucco, guarded the roof.
These decorations gave a modern appearance to the house,
but time had already planted the seed of decay therein : in
other words, a pipal seed had found its way into a little crack
above the doorway, and had spread and grown into a tree,
whose vigorous life waged war with the resisting bricks and
mortar. The grandeur of the exterior might lead one to
expect luxury within, but it was not so. A courtyard, cattle,
walls covered with manure, stuck on in round patches to dry
for fuel—this was the vestibule which led to a small inner
court, at one end of which was the cooking place. A couple of
rooms opened into a grateful gloom, and a narrow stair, white
and burning in the sunlight, seemed to lead right up into the
brilliant blue.

The first to appear was the lady of the house, who busied
herself in a leisurely manner amongst the cooking vessels—for
a while alone. Then, the thought of help suggesting itself, she
stood in the middle of the little court and, looking up to the
roof, called,—

"Chandkor! "

No one answered.

"The lazy child!" she muttered ; then, putting her hands
to her sides, she called more loudly,—

"Ni! Chandkoria!"

But she had to return to her work unaided.

The sun rose higher, and with the day came calls from the
outer world. The sweeper came with a vessel for the daily
wage of sour milk and a cake of bread. The food was not
ready, so she proceeded to sweep the floor instead, putting all
the accumulated rubbish of the night into her basket. A
servant came with a request, and finally two sons with very
dirty faces, which she washed with a glass of water! They

screwed up their cheeks into hard knobs and endured the operation patiently, even the valedictory slap which she administered on the wet shining surface as she bade them be off to their work.

All this time a gentle voice had asked for admittance at the shut door, but it was only when the knights of the washed countenances opened it to go out that the patient figure was seen.

"May I come in?"

"Come in, lady," said the sweeper, standing up with the basket of dust and rubbish on her head, and clinging close to the wall, so that none of her garments should touch the visitor. "Come," she repeated, seeing the lady hesitate because the hostess gave no sign of welcome.

Miss Gray, taking silence for consent, passed in and sat down in the narrow strip of shade facing the staircase.

She looked up to the dazzling blue, with the shrinking eyes of the North, while the daughter of the Sun looked at her now and then with indifference as she went on with her work.

"What does she come for? we don't want to listen to her story, it is *always* the same."

"I am very thirsty," said her visitor, breaking the silence which was becoming oppressive.

"Have you a vessel?"

"No."

"Use mine, lady!" The sweeper in her innate kindliness forgot for the moment that she was an outcaste.

It looked dirty, as indeed it was, and the lady paused—just for a moment. As she did so she forgot thirst and everything else, for, coming towards her from the upper room, she saw Chandkor—Chandkor, Moon Princess—whom her mother scolded for being late, but who was, for those who had eyes to see, a queen of women, and fair as the moon whose name

she bore.   Regardless of maternal reproaches, and evidently
unconscious of them, she sat down and looked at the stranger
with quiet interest.

"Surely those wonderful eyes long to look at something
higher than village life," thought Miss Gray.   As a matter of
fact the Princess of the Moon was wondering why her visitor's
eyes were so like the eyes of a cat!

"May I sing to you?"   Miss Gray had been thinking how
she should begin, and had decided upon opening with a hymn.

Chandkor nodded assent, so Miss Gray sang a few verses of
a favourite Indian air.

> "There is sorrow upon sorrow in the world;
>   The shadow of storms is everywhere.
>   Lord Jesus, come; why tarriest Thou?"

As yet, this Moon Princess knew little of sorrow—it was but
a name to her.   She had shed tears plentifully, but they had
not scalded her heart; so nothing in her was stirred by the
words of the hymn, further than her love for music.

"I like it very much," she said.

Miss Gray smiled and then told the beautiful girl of a balm
for sorrow and a Friend who loveth at all times.   Chandkor
listened quietly and gravely to the end, after which Miss Gray
took leave of her and went to the next house of call.

The sun had by this time mounted high in the heavens,
and was filling the courtyard of Bholā Singh with heat and
glare.   A woman was seated in the doorway grinding wheat,
but she stopped for a moment to wipe her tired, hot face as
Miss Gray entered.

"Is your work nearly done, Bibi?" inquired Miss Gray.

The woman smiled, and pointing to a heap of grain on the
floor said, "About half, lady! But what can one do? Twenty
sers (forty lbs.) to grind and fifteen sers to cook are our work
day by day."   She paused as if to rest for a while, but seeing

the mistress of the house coming out, she seized the handle and proceeded to move the heavy millstone with renewed vigour.

Miss Gray went forward to greet Bibi Kishen Dei, who, although pleased to see her, seemed to be overwhelmed with duties.

"What a time to come!" she cried; "neither time to sit down nor time to stand!" but added with a good-natured laugh, as she dragged a charpāi towards the less sunny part of the court, "Sit down. I shall come and sit by you directly"; and she hurried off, jingling as she went, for from the top of her grey head to the sole of her dusty foot she was laden with jewels. Heavy silver ornaments hung over the forehead and dangled in the ears, a massive necklet of one piece of solid silver, two great armlets worn over the sleeve of her jacket above the elbow, besides anklets, rings and toe rings, such are a few details of a Sikh lady's toilette!

Miss Gray sat down on the charpāi near which Bibi Bhāg Dei, the quiet and depressed daughter-in-law of the house, was sitting spinning. The little woman looked pleased but was silent, so Miss Gray had the conversation in her own hands until the baby, hitherto invisible, asserted himself by a kick, which twisted the "takla" of the spinning wheel, followed by a screaming when he saw that the wheel got more attention than himself.

The poor mother tried in vain to straighten the twisted needle with the howler on her lap, but had to give in at last. It was clearly impossible to do two things at once!

"Do give him to me!" said Miss Gray.

Bibi Bhāg Dei shook her head with the indulgent smile of the expert to the amateur in baby-tending. "He won't go," she said. She was much in need of help, but none seemed at hand; all her noisy but willing children had disappeared— the yard was empty. Looking up, however, she saw the face of a girl, presumably good-natured, leaning over the wall, so with a beseeching "Ah! Queen of ladies!" she proceeded to hoist Master Baby upwards. But the girl disappeared, and baby tumbled back again speechless for a short space into his mother's arms. Just then a child of about seven years scrambled down a ladder, and seizing the child, comforted it after the manner of small sisters, while she stared at the stranger all the time. "My name is Durgi," she said in answer to Miss Gray's question, and feeling on more intimate terms after this information, she sat down and began to examine the contents of the strange bag of books on the ground.

"Is Durgi the eldest child?"

"Yes," replied the mother, now absorbed in mending her wheel; then added, with more interest in her tone, "She is getting old; she must get married soon."

Bibi Kishen Dei had now joined the group, and at once demanded a hymn to be sung with the concertina. This she implied by an encouraging smile and a movement of her two hands to represent the playing of the instrument.

Miss Gray sang very well indeed, and her audience increased gradually. A few more children appeared—they seemed to have sprung up from the ground; two Muhamadan women, and the sweeper woman who had been grinding the corn, all gathered round to listen. But the singing was brought to a sudden stop. If a thunderbolt had fallen from the blue there could not have been more consternation. The Muhamadans fled like frightened hares, and Bibi Bhāg Dei covered her face with her chadar. Looking round, Miss Gray saw a tall, fat man, the cause of the panic, standing beside the charpāi. Attracted by the music, he had come silently forward, and now stood in the contemplative attitude of a great cow. The similarity of his expression to that animal was heightened by the thoughtful manner in which he chewed a straw.

"Go away, Nihāl Singh," said Bibi Kishen Dei, and Nihāl
Singh departed, but with some reluctance and with many
backward glances, while chewing his straw.

Bibi Bhāg Dei uncovered her face with a sigh of relief,
and the Muhamadan ladies, who had not gone far away, came
back after many affectations of looking round to see that the
coast was clear.

"What a fright I got!" said one breathlessly.

"Never mind Nihāl Singh," said Kishen Dei amiably.
"He is only a *pashu*."

"Pashu" means a beast, but the word was used in this
instance more as a term of affection than in reproach, for
Nihāl Singh, although only a labouring boor, was the one son
of the family who tilled the fields and managed the well, and
was kindly withal—at least so said his wife Bhāg Dei, and her
opinion must be considered beyond dispute. The covering
of her face afore-mentioned denoted a wife's reverence for
her husband, not her fear of the man, and is one of the
immemorial customs of the East.

Miss Gray resumed the singing of the hymn, but the spell
was broken. The babies had remembered to cry, while their
elders and betters strayed about in the sun looking at each
other's ornaments. She tried to speak a few words to them
before leaving, but their thoughts were miles away.

"Where were you born?" they asked—*not* a question belonging to her subject!

"In England."

"Never! You are not English; you speak our language
just like one of us."

Miss Gray smiled. They had just the moment before
pleaded their utter inability to understand a word she said.

"You have been to Deviditta's house," said another. "His
daughter has followed you here."

Chandkor was standing by.

"Take her home and make a Christian of her!" cried one of the Muhamadans in a rude, jocular manner.

Miss Gray said nothing to this, and very soon left. She feared that the foolish words might do harm, but to her surprise she found Chandkor at the outer door waiting for her on her way out. The word "Christian" had not frightened her after all.

"I want to sing over the lines again you sang this morning," she said, and, with a voice as true as her teacher's, she sang—

"Why tarriest Thou? Come, Lord Jesus."

"Did I make any mistake?" she asked, with the simplicity of a child.

"None, dear! Not one. Always sing it thus, and the Lord Himself will listen," and Miss Gray left with the words ringing in her ears. The sound followed her like a clear stream through the burden and heat of the day, and Chandkor, all unknown to herself, had laid by, in a corner of her heart, a balm for a time of hurt and wounding.

CHAPTER II

DEVIDITTĀ, the owner of the stucco-fronted house, was a merchant by trade. He was the rich man of the village, but the house and his stout person were the sole signs thereof, as he elected to sit all day in poor garments on the floor of the little shop, the contents of which overflowed into the street owing to want of room inside. His work seemed to consist of sitting still, as few people apparently stopped to buy, and as these exceptions contributed little more than a copper at a time one might question the lucrativeness of it, but Deviditā increased in wealth as steadily as he increased in person.

His family history was common enough to escape remark, and was therefore typical. His eldest child, Chandkor, had but a cold welcome at her birth because she was not a boy, and if she had not been a small person of unusual vigour she could not have survived the criminal neglect which was the outcome of her parents' disappointment. On the contrary, she throve upon all the family omissions and commissions which surrounded her infant days with peril, and as soon as possible repaid the small trouble of her upbringing by becoming a capable nurse to the little ones who succeeded her. She did what she could, this child with the baby face and brilliant eyes, seizing the unhappy infant by its arm or leg (whichever came uppermost), patting the little back to induce sleep, or covering up the wide-open mouth to stifle its cries, while she played with her co-temporaries in the mud. And no one rebuked her, because—the two little ones who followed her into the world were, alas, *not* sons!

"Girls never die," said the mother, in answer to the remonstrance of a Zenāna visitor; "they live through anything. But boys die, *of course.*"

Girls do not always survive, nevertheless; and Chandkor lost both her little sisters. The first she did not remember: the last she could not forget. The poor baby had been fretful and tiresome for some days, and one morning seemed very weak and ill, but Chandkor (the nurse) took it about as usual in the sun and dust. She had just then no thought to spare for anything beyond a game of ball, so mechanically wiping off a few tears from the little face, she joined her companions on the flat, hard mud by the pond. The baby lay very quietly on her shoulder while she played with the ball, striking it up and down on the smooth ground.

Fifty . . . sixty . . . the ball bounds steadily under her hand, while a group of children squatting round watched its progress. The game was nearly played out, and Chandkor was the winner.

"Eighty-one, eighty-two," she went on breathlessly.

A lurch to one side nearly brought the ball to a standstill, and the baby fell forward; but it did not cry, and the ball was caught at the rebound.

On it went to the full number—"Ninety-nine, a hundred!"

"I have won!" she cried, looking up with shining eyes.

Remembering the baby, she looked at the head on her shoulder.

"It is asleep," said the children.

"Yes, she is sleeping," said Chandkor; but she felt uneasy, and carried it home. How heavy it seemed now!

The mother took the child, and said nothing; but a feeling of wrong-doing smote Chandkor's heart.

"Did I hurt her, I wonder, when she fell? But no, she didn't cry, and babies always cry when they are hurt."

Thus this little heart accused and defended itself at the bar of conscience ; and still the mother said nothing.

"Oh, mother, she is asleep ; she has been asleep all the time."

At last she turned, but Chandkor, fearing a blow, fled out of the house.

The baby indeed slept well !

Nothing more was said, and Chandkor asked no questions. It is possible that she might have forgotten all about it, but for an incident which happened a few days later.

While standing at the door, she saw a group of Khatri women carrying a little burden in their arms. It was a dead baby of about a week old. Chandkor followed. They carried it out into the plain, and laid it away in a hole in the sand, lit a few lamps, and chanted the Service for the Dead—the special service for a dead baby girl :—

> "Gur khāwin
> Puni kātin
> Âp na āwin
> Wir ghallin."
> (Eat sugar—spin cotton—don't come back—send a brother.)

"Don't come back again ! No, she mustn't come back," thought Chandkor, as she followed the women home again stopping now and then to pick up her little shoe, which tumbled off into the sand. She did not feel sad : she was only very quiet and full of wonder during the day.

"She mustn't come back ; nobody wants her," she murmured, as she sat playing at ball ; "but I think I'll go and see if the red rag is still on the top of the mound, and the little lamps round it."

So she wandered off, past the pond, along the path by the

tufts of cut pampas grass, out into the great waste of sand, where the saltpetre lies like snow.

There was a hollow where the mound had been, and all the little earthen lamps had gone out.

"She has gone right away, so she will never come back," thought Chandkor, as she went back to the village over the sand.

She was too young to realize the ghastly truth. The covering of sand had not been enough to protect the baby from beasts of prey, so the little one had found no rest, not even in the grave.

And yet the sun, on its way over the slope of the West, looked on many little graves lying safe and still, and green with grass and gracious rain and mothers' tears : the graves of dearly-loved sons and daughters laid to rest on the slopes of "Bether" till break of Day.

But this was a vision beyond her seeing, and it told her quite beyond belief, for to Chandkor

"She must not come back"

was the one line of the story of the dead sister which clung to her memory as the days went by.

And this daughter of the East grew up beautiful as a dream-princess amongst a people who paid no heed to her because she was a girl, and because her baby brothers, one after the other, filled her mother's heart. They were called respectively Gopāl Chand and Motī Lāl, and, notwithstanding parental petting and spoiling and over-feeding, reached men's estate without any severe illness, and were not altogether unworthy of their names.

And still the shop prospered ; the family safe groaned with rupees. Devidittā enjoyed the flattery which wealth brings ; his wife received the respect and admiration due to a head heavily weighted with gold ornaments ; while the pipal tree

rippled in green waves of leaves over the ever-widening rent
in the wall.

A stone's throw from Deviditta's house lies the "weri" or
farm-steading of Bhola Singh; that is to say, it is the house
where his family and cattle live—the fields being outside
the village. It is like all other houses of the kind: an open
yard surrounded by one-storied dwelling-rooms, all built of
sun-dried bricks and plastered over with mud. In the centre
and at one side are mangers for the buffaloes and cows. The
entrance is by a closed doorway, which opens into the village
street. In this anteroom there is usually a large wooden
bedstead, on which the gentlemen receive their visitors : the
inner court being reserved for the ladies and all live stock !

Bhola Singh had lived up to his name, which means simple.
Added years had brought age without wisdom, and grey hairs
without reverence. But he had affection instead, for no one
could help liking the sturdy old man with the heart of a child.
His wife, Kishen Dei, on the contrary, was a clever woman.
She had begun life with more than her share of shrewdness,
and with this talent she traded (being given ample scope by
her husband) till she became the leader of her clan, filling all
the offices which fell to her lot with ability. She was an indulgent wife to her weak husband, a fond mother to her sons, a
severe one to her daughters and daughter-in-law, and grand-
mother to all the village.

Their family consisted of three sons and two daughters.
The eldest, Nihal Singh, has been described already as the
labourer of the family. The second, Gulab Singh, a stalwart
youth of six feet two in height, had all the fighting instincts of
his race, and was on the eve of enlisting in a Sikh regiment at
the time when our story begins. The third, Khazan Singh,
who had the reputation of being clever, was sent to school.
Possibly the old pundit, who saw many things in the star

which shone at his birth, discovered promise of a mine of wealth and learning in the infant's bald head ; and so he was called *Khazān*, which means a treasury. He was at this time studying hard, learning Persian and English, with the hope of gaining a B.A. degree—the magic sesame which opens the treasuries of. wealth and success.

The two daughters, Santo and Wanto, aged respectively seven and nine, were of the unruly type of girlhood which is of more hindrance than help in a household, so they were seldom desired at home. But that is a detail: their presence was an offence, because, being still unmarried, they were the cause of much jeering to their father by his neighbours and relations.

They lived chiefly in the fields ; and what a happy life it was ! running out and in amongst the sugar-cane, picking and eating the soft green lentil pods or the fragrant "sāg" for supper, and playing by the well. Each season brought its special delights, and it never seemed too hot or too cold for these children of the open air. Nothing short of heavy rain could keep them indoors, for there they had to endure irksome hours of spinning and household work, never well enough done to call forth praise, always apparently earning rebuke.

Thus passed the short dawn of their life, so soon to break into the full day of their married years.

Such, then, is the household of which Bholā Singh is the nominal head. It has its joys and sorrows and hard times, but he takes it all with the buoyancy of youth, which lives only in to-day. If he thinks of the future, it is of the time when Khazān Singh, having become *tahsildār*,[1] shall fill the family coffers with wealth. In the meanwhile he is poor : not all the frugality and ability of Kishen Dei can prevent this. Bholā Singh is poor and increases in poverty, as Devidittā is

[1] Deputy Magistrate and Sub-Collector.

rich and increases in wealth ; and they form a contrast in
worldly estate, as they do in mental gifts—innocence *versus*
treachery—while they live side by side.   Their paths were
to cross later on, but for the present they lived during the
hot season apart.   The fly may enjoy a long time of free-
dom, until, by the attracting power of the strong to the weak,
it falls into the spider's web.

CHAPTER III

THE time drew near when Gulāb Singh must leave home to enter on his military career. The recruiting sergeant had filled up the squad which he had been instructed to obtain, and the young men were all to start on their life's work. It was arranged that they should proceed *via* Amritsar. In order to combine business with pleasure, they so timed the journey as to spend a couple of days in that holy city at the time of the Diwālī fair, which occurs every year at the November new moon, so that the darkest night may be secured for the illuminations which accompany the feast. But there was a deeper object than merely seeing the illuminations which led the feet of the young soldiers thither. Amritsar is the sacred city of the Sikh race, the scene where their great militant Guru or leader, named Govind Singh, some centuries ago had chosen to make his hermitage, and which has ever since been the focus of Sikh religious life. It was necessary that in this sacred spot Gulāb Singh and his comrades should go through the ceremony of initiation called "taking the Pāhul." It may be taken anywhere, and any number of times during one's life, but if possible should be first taken in Amritsar.

It was a lovely evening as the party drew near. The young corn was growing strong and vigorous all over the flat country on either side of the dusty highway. But for the exceptions to be now noted, there was one vast sheet of deepest green to refresh the eye as far as the view could extend. The exceptions were that occasionally one could detect a faint tinge of

RUSTIC SUGAR PRESS ON THE LEFT, SHED FOR BOILING CANE JUICE ON THE RIGHT.

yellow, where the mustard crop was coming into flower, and filling the air with its sweet perfume. Or, again, there was the graceful sugar-cane in not infrequent patches, carefully fenced with thorn hedges, tied together with rude cords made out of its leaves, to protect its luscious foliage from the attacks of the thousands of cattle of every species now crowding the road on their way to the fair. The pressing of the cane for the extraction of its juice had already begun, and from the rude sheds near the field could be detected a thin wisp of smoke rising and diffusing an agreeable scent of the boiling juice. At one of these sheds the party halted, and the sergeant called out, "I say, Khālsā jī, you have a magnificent stock of cane here. The Sat Guru's blessing be on you, Wāh Guru; what a rich man you will be! What a magnificent pair of bullocks you will be buying at the Diwālī fair to-morrow from the proceeds of this fine crop!"

"Yes, brother," was the owner's reply; "but alas! it is not mine now. You know the seasons have been bad. The cattle-plague carried off my best teams last year, so that I have had to cultivate my land with hired oxen, and mortgage the produce in advance to the usurer. If I get the value of a quilt for this winter out of my fine crop, it is all I can do. But," he added, with a twinkle in his eye, as he looked at the travel-stained squad, and divined the object of the sergeant's civil speech, "I dare say you lads would not refuse a drink of the cane-juice? You are welcome."

A good draught of the liquor, just about to be placed on the fire, far too cloying to the English taste, was readily accepted by all the thirsty souls, who soon moved on, as they still had six miles to walk.

After three or four more miles the road suddenly rose, and they found themselves crossing a fine masonry bridge. "This," said the sergeant, "is the Canal. It comes from the Rāvī river, at the place where it issues from the high mountains,

and the Government has spent millions of money on carrying
it where it is needed. You know its waters, as they run in
tiny streamlets through your native villages. Here you see
one of the main streams ; how smoothly and evenly it glides
to gladden the thirsty wastes of the distant Bar. And look,
there is Amritsar, peeping through the trees which line the
road." The lads saw before them a glimpse of a tower, but
the foliage hid all else. On nearer approach, however, they
passed a fine set of buildings, which they learnt was a tank
and its surroundings, built by a rich merchant as atonement
for his sins. It consisted of a temple or two, one for the
Sikhs, and one for the Hindus, a set of alcoves, in which
travellers might sit during the heat, or even spend a night
when the weather was not too cold, and then the fine sheet
of an acre or two covered with water, to which flights of
masonry steps led down on every side of the square. At this
time of day there was only one wayfarer washing his feet, but
in the morning the scene would be one of great animation,
with multitudes of persons of all ages seeking to wash away
the moral as well as the physical defilements, of which they
were painfully aware. A few yards farther, and the party
reached the gateway, and passing under it, found themselves
in Amritsar. They pressed on past great timber-yards, stacked
with planks of the fragrant deodar, or huge piles of firewood
of the common acacia, through lanes of varying width, varying
odours, and varying styles of architecture, past the shops, the
sights and sounds of a city of 120,000 inhabitants, to a Būngā.
But what is a Būngā ? It is a sort of monastery, if that can be
so styled which contains no monks, but only a party of men
who come and go as they please, are under no mutual obliga-
tions, where there is no prior or other head, and probably only
a small endowment. At any rate, there is room to lie down on
a clean floor, and any good Sikh can gain admittance for a day
or two, and is welcome. It faced the great sacred tank known

as Amrit-sar. These words signify the " Pool of Immortality."
It is surely one of the most picturesque scenes in the world,
and under the designation of the Golden Temple is well known
to tourists, and to those who have seen a lantern show of
Panjab Missions. The Būngā where our party lodged was one
of those which look toward the Bāwā Atal, the Sikh West-
minster Abbey, where the cremated ashes of their mighty dead
are laid to rest. In the immediate foreground stretched the
pure white marble pavement which surrounds the sheet of
water on every side. To the left rose the two red sandstone
minarets of the Būngā belonging to the Rāmgarhia chiefs,
from the summit of which the lads next morning viewed the
expanse of housetops and palaces of the busy hive. Just in
front lay the superb edifice of the Golden Temple, on an island
save where it is connected with the mainland by a causeway of
purest white marble, flanked by tall marble lamp-posts. From
the distance where the young men saw it they could but faintly
discern the intricate and delicate tracery of cornelian, jasper,
and agate, in which the forms of birds, fruit, and flowers are
inlaid into the snowy marble walls of the building. At a
height of about eight feet from the pavement of the ambula-
tory surrounding the shrine commences the material which
gives its name to the temple, the sheets of gilt copper which
continue to the top of its walls, and at the four corners end in
exquisite cupolas, each covered with the same burnished gold.
To the right lay the magnificent gateway leading on to the
causeway, by which alone the worshipper can reach the shrine.
Beyond the massive height of this gateway were grouped a few
majestic trees, between the leafage of which could be faintly
discerned the irregular pile of the Akāl-Būnga or Deathless
Fane. Here it was that the lads were to resort on the morrow
for the ceremony of admission to the warlike Sikh Brother-
hood.

They slept so soundly that the sergeant had much ado to

shake them out of their slumbers before dawn to witness an
unwonted sight.   Rushing to the lattice, they beheld a procession of singers and musicians proceeding along the causeway
from the gateway to the temple.   Flambeaux were burning
around the central object, and though the sky was brilliantly
clear the marble was seen to be streaming with the water
which the temple guards had used during the night to purify
the whole precincts from the soiling caused by the bare feet of
the tens of thousands of worshippers who had trodden those
courts during the previous day.   The custom of going barefoot
upon the sacred marble is very trying in the cold winter morn-
ings, as the tour occupies about twenty minutes.   The central
object of the procession was a litter decked with flags, and
tinsel, containing a heavy pile of finest muslin.   But the gazers
were informed that beneath that muslin lay the Holy Granth
or Book, enwrapped in its many coverings of broadcloth, satin,
silk, cambric, velvet, and brocade.   " Now is the time," cried
their leader, " for us all to visit the Guru's shrine, and pay our
devotions at the beginning of this sacred day."   Each man
hastily twisted up his long hair (for no Sikh ever allows scissors
or razor to touch him from the day of his birth to his death),
and huddling on their simple attire they hastened to the gate.
Its name is the Gate of Vision (Darshanī darwāza).   Through
it alone could access be gained along the causeway, already
crowded to suffocation.   Along this causeway the party paced,
till they reverently bowed low as they entered the portal of the
temple itself, and beheld the Holy Book lying on its lectern,
which was placed on the ground.   Behind it sat an aged
priest, whose exquisite grey beard swept down his snow-white
vesture.   They had just turned to the left by way of beginning
their circuit of the shrine, and had cast on to the white sheet
spread on the floor before the Book their humble offering of
a few coppers, when a hush went round, and they perceived
that the whole moving assembly was struck into awesome

silence, and that all were in the act of prostrating themselves on the floor. The band at the same instant ceased its thrumming on the guitars, its pounding of the drums, its harsh chanting of the sacred strains. Following the fashion, our party assumed the attitude of devotion, and as the door was blocked by the persons already within the verandahs, absolute silence began to reign. The voice of the priest alone was heard, as he very tenderly opened the folds of covering, and chanted from the Book a few of its mystic sentences in a tongue now imperfectly understood. At the end of certain versicles occurred the word Nānak, the name of the first Guru or spiritual leader, who lived in the sixteenth century of the Christian era. At every naming of this name the whole devout crowd murmured in a suppressed tone of deep respect, "Wāh Guru, Wāh Guru." The reading was but short, and as soon as it ceased the band again struck up, the worshippers moved round, always going from left to right, until they returned to the doorway, where, with a low reverence, and one more murmur of "Wāh Guru," they quietly moved back along the causeway. By this time the sun was tipping the minarets with gold, the Mohammedan and Christian population of the city was awake, the cattle had begun to rush madly through the narrow streets, to the danger of foot-passengers, and the lads were free to enjoy themselves till the afternoon.

They employed part of this period in a more than usually careful toilette. All the travel-stained garments were removed, the bath in the sacred tank was taken at the Dukh-bhanjani steps, so called because they are supposed to remove distress from all who dip themselves in the sacred water there. About four o'clock in the afternoon the sergeant took his five lads to the Akāl-Būnga. They first were shown the weapons said to have been wielded by the mighty men of days gone by—the enormous two-handed sword, the mace with its frightful knobs of steel, the razor-like double-bladed dagger, the lithe and

piercing scimitar, the heavy sabre, each with its legend of
prowess to stimulate the youthful aspirant to fame. This
done, they divested themselves of all raiment save a slight
covering for the long hair of the head, and a pair of short
trousers, and took their stand on a marble pavement at the
foot of an elevated terrace, whereon sat three priests of the
faith.   In the hand of one of these was an iron bowl, containing water newly drawn from the sacred tank hard by.   In it
had been mingled a little crude brown sugar, and it was stirred
with a sword in the presence of the candidates.   The priest
then rose, and turning to the west, held the bowl high above
his head, reciting the passage out of the Japji (a portion of
the Sacred Books) suitable to the occasion.   He then handed
the vessel to his fellow, who went through the same ceremony,
and he handed it to the third, by whom this was repeated.
The principal officiant then violently sprinkled the faces of
the candidates with this sticky, thickened liquid, and as they
naturally flinched he chided them severely, saying, "If you are
afraid of a little water, how do you expect to face the shot and
shell when they whistle round you ?   Be men, stand firm, never
deny your faith, be courageous, pure, and trusty, never smoke
tobacco, remember the Guru, remember your Sikhism, be true
to your oath to the Government, and never flinch in the hour
of danger."   This done he gave the remains of the water to
be drunk by all out of the same vessel, and the ceremony
was concluded by all of them sitting down and eating together,
in token of undying unity, out of another iron bowl, a sort of
pudding made of flour, molasses, and spice.   After this they
were considered Singhs, or Lions.   But each was bidden to
be always provided with five things, the name of each of which
begins with the letter K :—Kachh, a short sort of body garment, answering to the English drawers ; this to distinguish a
Sikh from easy-going persons who encumber themselves with
flowing robes. Kanghi, or comb. Kara, or iron bracelet, to

be a memento that they are to be men of blood and iron. Karg, a miniature sword, which is usually worn tucked into the long hair. Kes, the long hair itself. It is necessary, they were told, for a man to keep his head hot with long hair, else where can be the valour?

In all this the Christian reader will not fail to see the many analogies to Christianity. The one Gate of Vision, by which alone can access be gained to the inner shrine, is an obvious parable (all unintended, but fitly suitable for use) of HIM who is the Door, and the Causeway of HIM who is the Way. In the ceremonial purity of frequent washings we see the natural yearning of all nations for inward cleansing. In the strange travesties of Baptism, and of the Holy Communion, we have traces in all likelihood of the teaching carried into India by Roman Catholic or Protestant teachers during the fifteenth and sixteenth centuries. The missionary can work from these lower considerations to the higher, which suggest themselves at every turn.

Returning to their Būngā, the young men for the first time observed that they had not had a bedstead to lie on, nor even any chair or stool, and were told that all these houses facing the sacred tank were destitute of bedsteads or stools, "For how can any one," said their leader, "think of elevating himself above the Sacred Book which is on its low lectern, and which is carried back at night with a like procession to that which you witnessed this morning to its bedstead in the recesses of the Akāl-Būnga? While it has a bedstead we may not venture to emulate it." This is another example which might be used to illustrate the letter which killeth.

At last the long, strange day drew to a close, and the young men sauntered about in the gardens of the "Kawal Sar" (the lotus pond), while the light, which is never allowed to go out, burned more clearly in the "Bāba Atal." They stared at everything with the eagerness of children, enjoying every nook and alley, and the sight of crowds of well-dressed towns-folk who had turned out as on a gala day.

The sergeant could hardly keep abreast of their questions, and at last advised them to reserve their eyes for the illumination at night.

"We always have a fine illumination in our village during the Diwāli," said Gulāb Singh.

The sergeant laughed. "Wait a bit," he said; "and after you have compared the two, let me know which you admire most—Amritsar, or Maure by the light of the Feast of Lanterns. But while we wait we had better have our evening meal."

Some time elapsed before they went out again, when the illumination was at its height. The night was dark, so the light which came from thousands of lamps shone with dazzling lustre. The temple was outlined in light, and the tall houses round the tank, and as far as one could see, wore crowns and garlands of brightness. It was as if with the day the town had laid aside all connection with work and reality, and had become a city of stars instead.

Gulāb Singh and his companions were struck dumb with astonishment. When they at last found utterance, it was to declare that it was like heaven.

"You could scarcely believe that all this splendour is but a number of little earthen lamps alit—just such lamps as you use at home," said the sergeant.

But at that moment the fireworks began. First a rocket went up, which fell back to the earth again in a golden rain; then a pillar of fire, which resolved itself into a crown; lastly, balls of various colours, which burst with a thunderous noise making the lads laugh for joy. So delighted were they that not until the lights began to flicker and go out could they be persuaded to go to bed. And older and wiser than they had enjoyed the scene: crowds of visitors—Indian and

English—sat by the sacred tank to watch the lights of Lakhshmi. Nor could a more brilliant sight be imagined, and all from little lamps of mud. A treasure in earthen vessels, bringing light and joy during the dark night.

CHAPTER IV

THE hundreds of pigeons, which the unearthly explosions and ghostly shimmerings of the sky rockets on the roof of the Golden Temple had terrified overnight, had barely settled themselves to roost in the small hours, when the ruddy dawn and the braying of the drums and trumpets of the Granth Procession again aroused them, and with them aroused the 200,000 people.

The sergeant had to attend the Government Treasury to get his cheque cashed for travelling expenses of his recruits to their distant military station. The train which British enterprise had brought to the doors of the sacred old-world city did not start till noon. The youths were therefore allowed by their leader to amuse themselves for an hour or two by a visit to the cattle fair, at a distance of a mile or so from the city along the Jullunder road. After a cold collation consisting for each of an unleavened cake of maize bread from last night's baking, and two-penny-worth of greasy sweetmeats from the nearest confectioner's, they sallied forth through the Rāmbāgh gate, which still retained some of the martial aspect which had been conferred on it in the days when Amritsar was a fortified city.

Within the streets and along the roads in its immediate vicinity the ground was moistened by men carrying the goat-skin bags full of water which are familiar to all Eastern travellers. But once beyond the gateways the dust and flies reign supreme, and on this foggy November morning the murky atmosphere was thick indeed. As the lads emerged from the gate, they spied a building, unlike any they had ever beheld, set back two or three paces from the road. They were informed that it was the Christian Church, the place of the worship of the Angrez log (English people), who now rule this country and kill cows for food. This was a thought so disgusting and awful that the lads were only too glad to forget it in the bustle of their unwonted surroundings. They hurried on, soon coming to a lamentable sight.

An ekka, or one-horse gig, lay upset over the embankment, with its load of four women, one boy, and two little girls all sprawling in the dust. One of the children was seriously hurt, as the bamboo canopy, with its heavy drapery, had fallen across her leg and cut it deeply. An excited colloquy was going on as to the disposal of the sufferer, and the further progress of the whole party. As it turned out that they were only low-caste Mohammedans, viz., shoe-makers and oil-pressers, the five young Singhs, in the pride of their recent baptism, went on, with the comforting conviction that after all there was some Power in the unseen world which took just vengeance on those who slay cows for food, as these sinners would do if they could.

On approach to the fair, the youths were astonished at the hubbub caused by the tens of thousands of oxen, cows, buffaloes, ponies, with a sprinkling of asses, camels, and goats, all supported by the running accompaniment of screams from excited drovers and angry bargainers. Amidst it all the recruits heard the strains of a well-known air. Turning a look to the right they saw a tent with a space rudely roped off, hard by the road. The area thus guarded was surrounded by a throng of listeners. The lads were tall, and easily looked over the shoulders of the crowd.

A well-dressed man was standing leading the singing, which died into silence as they drew nigh. The single voice, which then broke on the ear, began describing a family whose two sons were of opposite characters, one obedient to his father, the other perverse. The latter soon left home, and, going afar off, disgraced himself, and came to penury, which lasted till a better mind drove him back, to his father's delight, and his own reformation. So far it was easy enough to understand, but when the speaker urged from this simple narrative the lessons which all Christians draw from the parable, the astonishment of our listeners knew no bounds. They forgot the fair and its attractions, and became still more deeply interested, when a valiant champion of their own faith attacked the argument with these words, "Ah! you Christians, I know you. You have brought us some very good things. We get letters in two days from our sons afar off at the expense of only a halfpenny; we can also send and find out by your wonderful wires what are the prices of corn this morning in Karachi, which is 850 miles off, or in Bombay, which is 1,400 miles away. We know you mean to do justice, and to love mercy; but you are the impious destroyers of our cows. So long as you persist in such shocking ruthlessness, what wonder is it if we suffer under famine, plague, and rinderpest? How can the Deity possibly overlook such awful sin?"

He was interrupted by a Mohammedan, who roared out, "Ah! I like a good beef curry as much as they do, but I'm sure I'd never eat it out of their filthy dishes. Why, they eat those detestable evil things, and they drink the accursed wine and spirits which turn man into a beast. That is their whole creed. They eat the evil thing, and are as unclean as it is." (He would not defile his lips by bringing the word for pig on to them, so used the euphemism "bad," which means the same as it does in English—bad.)

Another opponent of a different colour of religious opinion interjected a query, which he considered would crush the whole Christian fabric into nothingness. "You Christians know that your deity, Jesus, once demeaned himself to take away a poor man's ass without paying for it, and another time cursed a poor man's fig tree. Are such actions fit to be imitated?"

To these objectors there was no time to answer, till the Christian cause was championed by an elderly personage of imposing mien and grave gesture, named Hosea, a well-known member of the Lahore staff, who had come over to Amritsar to take part in the customary preaching at the Diwālī Fair. His appearance was the signal for a temporary lull in the cross-fire of banter and scorn which had succeeded the explanation of the parable.

He quietly reminded the audience that it was not an occasion for revilings, or discussions about food, but that the question was by what means a sinless Creator could be reconciled to sinful man.

He had not been speaking for more than five minutes when the same Mohammedan broke in. "God is all-merciful; He will surely forgive the peccadilloes of any who will say that he repents."

While Hosea was pointing out in answer that such an argument subverts the truth and justice of One who can by no means clear the guilty, a brawny Sikh interrupted him with these words, "Well, I don't know what sense there is in a word you say. When everybody knows that all our actions are written on our foreheads before we are born, and when we know *kartā karātā āphī āp* (He Himself causes and He acts), what is the use of our attempting to do right? The Deity is the cause of it all. The Deity is everywhere—He is in my body, He is in my foot, He is in the shoe which covers my foot, He is in the ground which my shoe treads upon, He is in the air, He is all-pervading and all-arranging. There's an end of it. We are helpless."

A more logical listener rebuked him by observing that this

theory would make the Deity to be the author of all evil, and the cause of suffering to innocent persons despoiled of honour, property, or life by the adulterer, the robber, or the man-slayer.

While this conversation was proceeding in front of the preaching tent, a hot argument had been started in a corner of the crowd between an adherent of the Brahmo Somāj, who was volubly urging that God has revealed Himself to man, but not exclusively to any one man, and a member of the Aryā Sāmāj, who was extolling the Vedas as the true vehicle of inspired utterance. The former stated his position thus:

"Confucius in China, Mohammed in Mecca, Jesus in Eng-land, Bāwā Nānak in the Panjab, Chaitanya in Bengal, Bāwā Kabīr in Ujain, Gautama Buddha in Bombay, all were men who had light. It is the part of a wise man to select from their writings whatever is true and valuable, to believe it, and act upon it. At the same time they were all human, and all made mistakes, so it is the part of the wise man not to take all they said for granted. Every man must think the subject out for himself. My motto is 'No one man, and no one book.'"

The Aryā replied, "Well then, sir, will you tell me a rule by which I am to select? It strikes me that you act as one would do who should receive a prescription from the physician containing six different ingredients, and should make up six different powders, combining the drugs in different propor-tions. We know that this would result in some of the powders being absolutely inert, while others would be deadly, and none would cure the invalid."

"You're a fool, sir," answered the Brahmo. "That is of course not my meaning. Of course, a man must have common sense, and not take from the various teachers any more of each than he can assimilate."

"My opinion is, sir, that you are a bigger fool than I to pro-

pose such a stupid method of solving the great difficulties of
religion."

This warm contention drew all the crowd to listen to the
combatants, who rose in their agitation and departed, while the
disappointed Christians started a new hymn to attract a quieter
audience.

It had ceased. The next preacher was describing the
Divine plan of salvation, when a good-natured grocer observed,
"Surely, sir, it is a little uncharitable in you to assert that your
way is the only way. We have never heard of this religion of
yours, till the last fifty years. What has become of all our
forefathers? Do you not know that people have come in
tens of thousands to Amritsar the last three days, from all
quarters, and have entered the city by whichever one of its
thirteen gates was nearest? The gates were different, but
the people all got into Amritsar. So we shall all get into
Paradise—you by your way, I by mine, this Mohammedan
friend of mine by his. What is the use of all this declama-
tion?"

"My brother," was the answer, "it is quite true what you
say. But when you have got into Amritsar, where are you?
You cannot call it a saintly place. There are in it thieves,
gamblers, cheats, virtuous persons, rich and poor, sirdars, and
beggars, all mixed up together. But Paradise is a place, as
you will allow, where nothing unclean or evil can enter. Let
me remind you that when you went to bow your head this
morning at the Golden Temple you did not swim to it."

"No, of course not; I went in by the Darshanī darwāza—
that is the only way in there."

"Very well; now you will say that the temple is a sacred
spot, and its frequenters are, or are supposed to be at any rate,
well-meaning and trustworthy persons. Surely that is a better
emblem of Paradise, is it not?"

"Well, I suppose it is."

" But there is only one way in there.   So Christ is the one way of access to the Father of us all."

This little simile struck the young Khatri, and he sat down to hear a little more of this one way, for he was a sincere young fellow, who had long felt dissatisfied with the husks of the Hindu belief.   After a lengthy talk by him and the four or five other peaceable ones who had squatted on the carpet beside him, he took his leave, and accepted two or three short treatises explaining the principal doctrines of the Christian faith, by means of parables and quotations from the Granth with comments.   The young English missionary who had been present all this morning and had understood most of the simple talk, though not yet able to discourse himself, heaved a sigh as he saw his last audience melt away into the fair. " Well, the word of GOD says, ' Blessed are ye who sow beside all waters.'   We have striven to do our part.   Let us unite in asking for a spirit of inquiry to enter that last young fellow's mind and to lead him to Christ."

The little band bowed their knees in prayer to the idle wonderment of the passers-by, and then left for their day's work, till the afternoon coolness should permit them to sally forth again.

CHAPTER V

ABOUT a year after his enlistment Gulāb Singh's regiment was ordered off to British Central Africa, and Bibi Kishen Dei, who had until then been proud and pleased to be the mother of a soldier of the Queen, saw him go with a sinking heart. She had but now realized that honour and glory bring separation and perhaps death in their train. Many a time during the first days of his absence, she would go out and gaze over the fields of millet and maize towards the sinking sun and weep as David for Absalom.

"My son has gone to the *town* of Africa," she said to Miss Gray, who called a few days after his departure. "That is many days' journey into your country, is it not?"

"Not quite so far, Bibi." (It was impossible to give further particulars to one who believed everything out of the Panjab to be England!)

"Ah! but he has gone out of my sight and hearing!"

"But he will come back again."

"Yes, he will come back, but in the meanwhile his old mother may die!"

Bibi Kishen Dei was spinning swiftly, but her well-practised fingers guided the thread without the aid of the eyes, which at that moment were blind with tears. Her chadar had fallen off and the merciless sun beat upon her careworn face, but she gave no heed, until seeing a little buffalo calf lying, panting with heat, she drew her chadar over her eyes, and rising up, untied the little creature and brought it into the shade.

"The poor thing can't speak. I can go out of the sun-
shine when I like, but it is tied!"

"May I come too, and sit beside the buffalo in the shade?"

"Ah, yes! I forgot," said Kishen Dei kindly. "You don't
like heat either, you worm of the snow!"

It was unusually hot during the middle of the day for the
time of year.

The little incident brought a smile to her face, which Miss
Gray was glad to see, but it was only the short passage of a
beam of light through rain.

The ever-turning wheel hummed as it followed Kishen Dei's
rapid fingers; but the thread broke oftener than its wont, and
as she stooped to mend it her tears fell fast.

"Have you seen my son Gulāb Singh?"

"No, but I have seen Nihāl Singh ——"

"*Nihāl Singh!* Having seen *him* cannot represent to you
the beauty of my soldier son, who in appearance is tall as a
camel and whose temper is sweet as ——"

Words failed to express its quality, so Miss Gray suggested
"sugar"—a simile evidently much to the lady's liking, as she
used it ever after!

At this juncture Bibi Bhāg Dei appeared rolling her spinning-
wheel before her; and Durgi with the baby strolled along the
yard, so Bibi Kishen Dei had to remember her position as
head of the family as well as being the mother of the son who
had gone away.

"Durgi!" called a faint voice from one of the inner rooms.
"Durgi!"

Durgi paid no heed; she was at that moment fingering Miss
Gray's hat—"to see if it was made of mud," she explained;
"it is just the colour of it."

"Durgi!" the voice again insisted.

"Go at once, Durgi," said Kishen Dei; "Khazān Singh
wants something."

Durgi sauntered towards the door with all the slowness of
the messenger who is as smoke to the eyes, stopping now and
again to point out some object of interest to the baby before
she disappeared into the room. Presently she came back, her
mind still fixed upon further investigation of the visitor's hat.

"What did Khazān Singh ask for?" inquired the grand-
mother.

"Water."

"Go at once and bring it," said Bibi Kishen Dei so severely
that the child ran off.

"Khazān Singh has had fever for six days. Will you give
him some medicine?"

The thought of an English remedy had only then occurred
to her.

"It is impossible to prescribe without seeing the patient;
besides, I only doctor women and children."

"Yes, yes, very proper, I am sure; but Khazān Singh is
but a boy—a mere infant. You cannot object to look at his
hand (*i.e.*, feel the pulse)."

So the doctor for women and children went and found the
mere infant a student of many arts and sciences, and conse-
quently very much a young man. He was very ill and very
uncomfortable, tossing under a quilt and with a turban half
uncoiled for a pillow, while a veritable plague of flies settled
upon his face. Poor lad! he was greatly in need of help, but
the lady doctor could do little more than feel his pulse, which
bounded and throbbed under the burning skin.

"It may be only remittent fever," she said to Bibi Kishen
Dei; "but you must be very careful. Give milk diet only and
the medicine which I will send."

"Not bread? We always give him bread (an unleavened cake)
and 'sāg' (boiled turnip tops), but to be sure he won't eat it."

It was a case of a strong constitution being tried to the
utmost. Bholā Singh bought a bottle of herb decoction from

the village apothecary, to which Bibi Kishen Dei added
another remedy on her own account.   This was supplemented
by the medicine from the Mission Dispensary, regardless of
the directions on the bottle.   It was to be administered in
specified quantities three times a day ; but upon the principle
that one can't have too much of a good thing, it was given in
liberal helpings, which emptied the bottle much sooner than
the doctor intended.   The barber came and rubbed the lad's
feet with oil, and the barber's wife recommended a patent
powder of her own to be given enveloped in a sweetmeat ; but
the fever yielded to none of them.   At last they consulted the
Prohit, who summed up the case to every one's satisfaction.

"All remedies have failed because no one has hitherto discovered the cause of the illness.   It is not fever, but an evil
spirit which clings to the lad.   Now the best way to remove
such a cause is to take Khazān Singh to a holy place where no
evil spirit can live."

"Yes, Mahārāj !" said Bholā Singh submissively.   "Where
shall I take him ? "

The Prohit thought for a moment.

"I should advise Govindwāl," he said.

Bholā Singh paid the consulting fee, and very soon the
removal was arranged.   The patient was taken as he was, on
his bed, which was slung to a pole and borne by two men.
So he was swayed along the dusty road accompanied by his
mother and sisters, father and brothers, and other relatives
whom for convenience' sake we may designate as cousins and
aunts.   Bibi Kishen Dei led the way, carrying her best red
cotton skirt bordered with green twisted in a knot on the top
of her head to keep it out of the dust.

By evening they came in sight of Govindwāl.   The sun was
sinking in glorious colours behind the trees ; the foreground,
bathed in a rich gloom, looked farther away than it really was,
for a few steps more brought them to the gate.

CHAPTER VI

MĀI PREMĪ was reading to a group of patients in the Govindwāl Dispensary verandah when our Maure friends arrived.

"I am Gulāb Singh's mother, and these"—pointing promiscuously towards the troop behind her—"are my relations. We come from Maure," she added, folding her skirts around her as she sat down.

Thus introduced the motley party sat down in detail—Bibi Bhāg Dei, her daughters Durgi and Jassi, and the baby, Santo and Wanto, a few small cousins and two elderly aunts.

Māi Premī looked a kind welcome through a pair of large horn-rimmed spectacles, and begged them to sit nearer her while she read.

"Come, dear children," she said, with a smile to the little ones. "Come and look at my pictures."

Santo and Wanto, who had never until that moment known themselves to be "*dear*," opened out under the new experience like flowers in the sun.

Māi Premī explained the meaning of the pictures, but she had not an attentive audience. They had come for medicine, and were on the alert for the tinkle of the bell which summoned them, one by one, indoors. The only exceptions were Bibi Bhāg Dei, who listened quietly all the time, and the little girls, who liked the novelty of being loved.

At last their turn came, and Bibi Kishen Dei, as became her age and position, went in first. She returned presently with a bottle.

"I suffer from rheumatism in the cold weather," she explained, "so this will come in usefully by-and-by. The lady doctor is very wise," she went on after a pause, "and old——"

"*Old!* ho! ho!" Māī Premī laughed heartily at the idea.

"Yes, old. Otherwise why should her hair have ripened like the wheat in May (*i.e.*, become white)?"

"It is the fair hair of the people of England, which I think beautiful," replied Māī Premī.

"Oh! She is still young! Young, but nevertheless wise, *very* wise," and Kishen Dei sighed deeply. "I told her that I had had fever for many days, that I could eat nothing, and that I was suffering from faintness and occasional delirium; but she gave me no medicine."

"You, in fact, described the symptoms of your husband or son."

"Yes," cried Kishen Dei, delighted at Māī Premī's sagacity. "You are very wise too. It was for my son, Khazān Singh."

"You should have told the truth, Bibi."

"My son is a piece of my heart, so it was no lie; but I knew beforehand that the 'Doctor Miss' would not understand this, as she gives medicine to women only."

"But there is a doctor for men in the town."

Bibi Kishen Dei settled into a confidential attitude. "She told me to take him to the men's hospital. Do they give proper remedies? Yes? Then perhaps I'll tell his father to go and see."

The other ladies of the party were in the meanwhile going into the consulting-room by turns, not apparently on account of present illness, but in the prudent spirit of the ant, which lays by a store for future need. Bibi Bhāg Dei appeared to be lost in thought.

"The lady doctor wears no jewels," she said, as she tied

up a packet of powders in the corner of her chadar. "Nothing in her ears, nor her nose, and no rings."

"What has *an old woman* to do with jewels?" said her mother-in-law severely.

In spite of Māī Premi's explanation, Kishen Dei reserved her right of private judgment, and so the fair-haired lady doctor was for ever, to her, one of the aged.

An hour after, Bholā Singh took his son to the men's dispensary.

The doctor listened patiently to the old man's vague story, and after seeing the patient, advised his staying in the hospital.

"The fever has left," he said; "change of air has been the best thing for him, but he needs care and feeding up."

Bholā Singh hesitated. Many difficulties suggested themselves in an incoherent way to his poor mind. "Khazān's mother would have known what to do," he reflected. The thought of her, however, brought an idea with it—a way of escape.

"If the emperor, so kind to the sick, will allow a slave to ask the opinion of his house—while the boy remains on the verandah——" he began.

The doctor saw at a glance that the fear of unclean food was weighing upon his mind; he saw, also, that no assurance to the contrary from himself would dispel the old man's doubts, without the sanction of his household, so he nodded a kind assent, and began to say a few comforting words to the lad.

Bholā Singh accordingly went to seek advice from his house—in other words, to consult Bibi Kishen Dei. It is etiquette to speak of a wife, not as a person, but as a building. Whatever may be the immediate reason thereof, it suggests the delicate compliment that she is the centre and shelter of the family.

D

Bibi Kishen Dei saw no objections to the scheme. The food difficulty was disposed of at once by her saying that she would cook for her son with her own hands, and watch him eat it.

"But if the doctor forbids bread?"

"Then I'll feed him on goat's milk, for you know cow's milk is too heating for a case of fever, or—do whatever the doctor says, but *I'll give it myself*, and then it will be all right."

Thus Kishen Dei decided the matter, and about a week later they had the pleasure of taking the invalid home restored.

The Prohit was delighted.

"I have never known a pilgrimage to fail," he said, with more enthusiasm than veracity.

Bholā Singh attributed the cure to the six days' reading of the Granth, for which he had paid many rupees. But Bibi Kishen Dei gave the honour to whom it was due. The opinion of a lady is more or less coloured by the thoughts of her heart, and Kishen Dei had been won over by the doctor.

"He shall never want 'sāg,'" she said, "as long as Kishen Dei can cook." And she kept her word. Many a time a mysterious message would bring the doctor out from amongst his bottles of medicine and crowds of patients to find Kishen Dei standing with a jar on her head.

"Just to show to you the grateful heart of Khazān Singh's mother. Stay, my son, and tell me how you are," she would say if she saw a sign of his departure. And Dr. Galens would talk to the kindly old Sikh woman to her heart's content, never considering the time thus spent lost to the work.

"The Queen is very good to spare us such a clever doctor," she remarked more than once, thereby increasing her own importance and his fame.

A PANJABI STREET.
A water-carrier, and father with child, buying clay toys.

CHAPTER VII

NOTHING distracts a Zenāna visitor more than the presence of men-folk. The women are not at ease, nor
is the teacher. Even should the male intruder be in sympathy
with the lesson—a rare instance, by the way—it is impossible
to go on with it *as usual*. The reader who has gone through
the ordeal of giving an object lesson in public will understand this. Miss Gray therefore did not welcome Khazān
Singh when he strolled up to the corner where she was
sitting with Bibi Bhāg Dei, with all the assurance of a suc-
cessful Government School student home for a holiday. The
training and environment of such schools and colleges very
often lead a man to "doubt everything in heaven and
earth but his own self." And Khazān Singh was not as yet
one of the many exceptions to this statement. That stern
step-mother called *Life* had not as yet taken him in hand
with her discipline of experience.

Bibi Bhāg Dei shrank into herself like a sea anemone when
he drew near.

"I wonder very much that you waste your precious time
upon the felt brains of such a woman!"

Bhāg Dei spun steadily. Her impassive head and face,
covered by the dingy chadar, seemed to merit the reproach—
and yet! but a minute before her poor plain face had been
beautiful when she asked her teacher if the Lord Jesus had
really waited during the heat of the day to talk to a woman.
Miss Gray's heart burned hot within her with a passionate

feeling of chivalry towards a dumb creature, hurt, albeit through want of thought, and words more scornful than Christian were ready to fly like sparks from the heated hearth, but she called them back in time. " He knows no better, poor lad," she thought ; then she told him gently that her pupil and she could learn best alone. But Khazān Singh, full of his own importance, had lifted up Miss Gray's Bible and was looking at it after the manner of the " Higher Criticism "!

" Have you read the Bible ?".

"Yes; indeed, I had one of my own. A preacher at Govindwāl gave it me, but the white ants ate most of it, so I threw it away. After all it did not signify. I prefer to read scientific books."

He laid down the Bible and went away.

Bibi Kishen Dei had not heard any of the conversation. She was not very well, and sat huddled up on a bed placed on a raised part of the yard in full blaze of the January sun. Her attention was fixed upon a fat Mohammedan beggar who had come in and was sitting on the edge of the daïs. He had a bag of flour filled by handfuls from the labourers, a bottle of oil and a piece of iron—a fortune-telling charm—of about twelve inches long. From it hung seven chains finished off into pointed ends.

" Will the medicine do me any good ?" inquired Kishen Dei of the oracle.

The faqir threw down the bunch of chains, looked at the direction in which they lay, then with his head on one side said very solemnly :

" Yes."

" When am I going to get well ? "

He threw the chains down once more, examined them, and said :

" In a month or two."

" How is Gulāb Singh ? "

Again the links fell on the ground, and after due examination of their position, he said :

"He is well."

"When will he write to me?"

"Soon," he replied, after deep thinking upon the chains.

Bibi Kishen Dei seemed to have an inexhaustible fund of questions, but the faqir changed the current of her thoughts by opening his flour bag with a pleading gesture. He wished it to be understood that he was very hungry.

"Give him what he wants," said Kishen Dei to Bhāg Dei, when she saw that she could ask no more. With a sigh and a shiver of cold, she wrapped herself in the well-worn quilt ; the sun, hot as it was, failed to comfort her.

Bibi Bhāg Dei rose at once and gave the faqir a large handful of flour, and yet another, as he was not satisfied.

Miss Gray sat down by Bibi Kishen Dei. "Do you really believe all the faqir says?"

She was surprised to find that Bibi Kishen Dei, so shrewdly suspicious of everything, should be so credulous. She had yet to learn that suspicion and credulity are the right and left hands of superstition.

Bibi Kishen Dei allowed the absurdity of it, remarking that such prophets always give good news when they receive good measure of wheat in return—(no dole at all would bring cursing)—but in her heart of hearts she believed in the message of the iron rod all the same.

The subject of conversation was interrupted for a little by the entrance of the Prohit's wife. She was a Brāhmanī, so Kishen Dei rose to offer her a seat.

"Has she come to help you?" asked Miss Gray.

"I come for what I get!" said the Prohit's wife with admirable honesty.

Bibi Kishen Dei smiled, a little sadly Miss Gray thought.

"Nothing for nothing in this world," she said.

" The best of all things is given us without price, Bibi ! "
Bibi Kishen Dei looked interested.

" What is it ? " she asked.

" The love of God."

Her interest died away.

" Yes, I know it, the great God above loves us; but I
don't want anything just now but the love of my son. Oh !
if I could but hear from him ; but no letter has come, and
he is so far away."

" Write and tell him so, Bibi," suggested Miss Gray.

" I have done so. The Pandit wrote for me, and I paid
him well, so that he should write good words ; but I have
had no reply."

" Shall I write another letter for you ? "

" Will you ? Will you write in *Gurmukhi*, so that he can
read it with his own eyes ? "

Bibi Kishen Dei was radiant.

" I'll fill a quilt for you with the softest cotton from the
fields. . . . I'll bring you milk. . . . I'll——"

" I want nothing, Bibi. I'll do it because I love you all,"
said Miss Gray, taking out note-book and pencil from her bag.
" Now tell me what to say."

" Tell him, tell my dear son Gulāb Singh, Laiz No. 62,
Company 1st——"

" *Slowly*, Bibi ! " cried Miss Gray, trying to stem the torrent
with one hand, while she wrote with the other.

Kishen Dei stopped for a minute, then resumed :

" Tell him that we are all well, that we wish him well,
that wheat is now selling at eight sers the rupee, that we are
many rupees in debt, that we wish him back, that his old
mother is ill, that his father is not very well——"

Miss Gray again begged for breathing space, but the flow of
words went on as the rivers of water !

" . . . That Santo and Wanto and Durgi must be

married, that his old mother keeps her dear son Gulāb Singh
in her heart—*just here.*" Kishen Dei paused to show the seat
of her affections. It was somewhere on her person near her
right arm, but *she* said it was her heart! " . . . His
father's salāms, his mother's salāms, Nihāl Singh's salāms, etc.,
etc." Each member of the large family was supposed to add
his and her salāms at the end.

" I'll post this at once," said Miss Gray when the epistle was
finished.

" Will you put it into an envelope ? "

"Yes."

"And address it *very* distinctly, so that there may be no
mistake. And . . ."—Bibi Kishen Dei looked anxiously
at her friend—" will you write upon the outside that the *boy
who carries the letter to Africa must not stop on the way ?* "

The Prohit's wife reminded her that more than *one* messenger must carry letters when the way is long.

" Yes," said Kishen Dei, " they lay a ' dāk ' (post) for distant
places—and "—reluctantly—" they may have to do so with this
letter, as it is a long, long way to *Africa town* ! "

" When will the answer come ? "

Miss Gray counted the time of going and coming, and
said that if he wrote by return Kishen Dei might have it by a
certain day.

As it happened Gulāb Singh wrote at once, and when his
mother got the letter at the time she had expected it her wonder and gratitude knew no bounds. And Miss Gray earned a
reputation which almost equalled that of the gentleman of the
iron links.

Taking leave of Kishen Dei, Miss Gray went to Devidittā's
house, hoping to see Chandkor, but she was disappointed.

" The star of women (Venus) set, so she returned to her
father-in-law's house," said her mother, who was as usual too
busy to sit down.

"Yes, she may come back"—in answer to Miss Gray's question—"but her home is in Amritsar. If you wish to see her you must go there."

Miss Gray felt sad and dispirited as she walked across the fields on her way home. Visions of work evidently useless, of battles fought at great odds, of faces which ranged themselves as friends and enemies in the warfare—Chandkor with her "wit above woman's and beauty of face," Bhāg Dei in her ignorance, Kishen Dei and the Mohammedan beggar—each shone and faded in turn in brightness or gloom, and as is the wont of the tired head the darkest colours remained the longest. The web of life and work seemed wholly black now that Chandkor had gone; but, silently, as she wove her dark threads a strand of gold was binding them together even while she knew it not.

The faqir meanwhile pursued his beggarly calling until the evening. Bhāg Dei sat at her wheel, wearily enough, but cheering her heart with the refrain which rose and fell with the thread :

"Come, Lord Jesus ; why tarriest Thou ? "

"I cannot sing it as Chandkor does," she thought, "but the Miss Sahib says that my poor voice can reach His ear all the same."

Kishen Dei's thoughts were winging their way to the strange land where her best-loved son was, but they were brighter thoughts now—not, as their wont, like sad-coloured swallows, but as flights of white birds, coming to and fro from the shining lands of hope. And Chandkor was receiving in her new home the love and appreciation which had been denied her amongst her own people.

Truly in our fear of evil we wrong our Father's thoughts of peace.

A RURAL SACRED TANK.

A rough imitation of the Golden Temple. (See Frontispiece.)

CHAPTER VIII

IN all village missions the cold weather, excepting the damp, misty weeks in January, is spent by missionaries in camp, so that the villages in the outlying district may be visited. The work, therefore, is not a daily routine amongst pupils, schools, and well-known village friends, but visits to little-known houses, preaching the word to " whosoever will." The medicine-chest, next to a box of books and tracts, is the most important of the means used ; the healing of the sick being the most sure way to win even the hardest hearts.

Miss Gray and her fellow-workers had had exceedingly busy, but not very encouraging, days, and it was with rather a sinking heart that she saw the towers of Rāmtīrath appear across the fields. The notes of it in the last year's diary, open before her, were not reassuring : "Rāmtīrath visited ; six houses. Hindu and Sikh—very bigoted. Could not get a hearing."

" Perhaps I shall be more fortunate to-day ; anyway, the place is interesting, whatever the people may be," and the " maiden " sent forth by " Wisdom " felt the joy of beauty as she walked through the quaint streets. They were refreshing to the eye because so unlike the usual type, for Rāmtīrath resembled more a miniature town than a village. The houses, which belonged for the most part to Sikh chiefs and rich moneylenders, were built of brick, and were of castellated form, none the less picturesque because falling into decay. Dark doors, beautifully carved, opened into dim corners ;

fretted balconies looked down over the street; a well, an old temple, and green glittering pipal leaves, each presented a study in itself as she passed by. At last, finding a doorway where a woman and a few girls' were spinning, she sat down. The house belonged to a Khatrī, so she waited outside until the lady should call her within. A little boy, who seemed to consist chiefly of a coat and two very fat legs, looked doubtfully in at the doorway where the stranger sat.

"Will she catch me?" he whispered to one of the girls.

Assured to the contrary, he came cautiously in; but his little heart misgave him, and he ran off crying,—

"Bebe! bebe! she is going to give me medicine!"

The bebe—that is his mother—brought him back with her to see the new comer. He sat for a while safely in her arms, in quiet enjoyment of wonder, till another fear crossed his mind,—

"Will she bite?" he asked.

Miss Gray told him that such was not her custom, but he did not seem to believe it. Possibly her solah topi (sun hat) was the cause, as it sometimes gives an alarming impression to unaccustomed eyes. Wishing to conciliate him, she took it off and held out her arms. It was a false step! Thinking that his worst fears were realized, he bounded indoors and shrieked, "There is *something!*—*something* going to—— !" then melting into tears, he lay kicking and sobbing on the floor.

This incident, apparently disastrous, was in fact the best thing that could have happened. The ladies of the house, who had no intention of disturbing themselves to come down from the sunny roof, ever so many steep stairs up, to see a person, thought differently when they heard that it was a thing —and possibly an awful thing! So one came down to see, and then another, till a goodly throng assembled. Miss Gray played a few notes on the concertina, and began to sing:

"Why tarriest Thou? Come, Lord Jesus."

They listened attentively, even the little boy, although the tears still trickled over his little dirty face.

When the hymn was done, to Miss Gray's surprise and pleasure she saw Chandkor.

"No one told me that you were here," she said, "but the sound of these words brought me. I think I should hear them even if I were dead."

"I am so glad I came to-day!"

"If you had not come to-day I should not have been here. I leave for Amritsar to-morrow. I have already stayed too long with my aunt; besides, one's own home is best, always best," she added with a smile.

She seemed to be very happy in the lot which had been cast in a pleasant place, but just then she was unusually silent and depressed.

"There is something I would like to tell you," she whispered; "but I cannot, they watch me so." One of the women looked suspiciously at her, so Miss Gray began to speak of the meaning of the hymn. Chandkor disappeared from the crowd, and Miss Gray had given up all hope of seeing her alone again; but on leaving the village she saw her by the well. No one was in sight.

Coming forward, she laid her hands on Miss Gray's shoulders, very much like a child in trouble. She seemed to have forgotten the fact that a Hindu may not touch an outcaste (all races are unclean to them).

"Sister, tell me one thing! Can one love the Lord all alone in one's heart, and no one know about it?"

"Light cannot be hid, dear."

"But—but must one *confess*? Oh, it is easy for you!" she cried—"so easy that you cannot know what it means to me. It means——"

Miss Gray could but know in part what it meant to Chand-kor, for the children who have "been ever with peaceful hearts in their Father's house" can never fully understand the peril and fear of those who enter in at a later hour.

"May God help you to do His will," was all she could say.

The angel of joy who comes with the tidings of a soul's awakening carries sometimes in his right hand a sword which pierceth the heart. Miss Gray saw more of the sword than the angel's face as she looked on the desolate figure by the well. But had she known all, she could not have doubted even for a moment the pity of the Father who remembereth that we are dust.

Was it a coincidence that on that evening Chandkor's husband, Prabhū Dās, resolved, after much conflict, to visit a friend—a Christian friend—who lived in a large house near the Golden Temple in Amritsar?

"If any one can help me, Ishwar Dās can," he thought. "I hope no one else is with him."

Mr. Ishwar Dās was alone, and for a while they sat together in *quasi* silence in an upper room, which overlooked the sea of houses.

"I have come to you for advice, or at least sympathy; but it is a difficult matter to explain," began Prabhū Dās at last.

His friend listened in kindly patience while the story was told with many pauses.

"To begin at the end, I am a Christian."

"Thank God," said Ishwar Dās.

These words, so often used, meant much to those two men that night, alone amongst the heathen.

"I heard the truth about a year and a half ago," he continued. "I heard it at the Diwālī fair from a young missionary. He made many mistakes in language; but I did not mind, because I saw that he was possessed by the Spirit of God. I have read of it since, and am persuaded, and believe, but the cost is more than I can pay—the cost of leaving *all* and following the Master. Is there no mercy with Him for such as I, who love Him so well in secret?"

"The command is that we must confess Him before men. You know the alternative."

"Yes; but the cost of it! My mother will be broken-hearted; my relations will desert me. . . . Does the Master wish that such as I should be left alone?"

"What about your wife?"

"I dare not tell her, because I dare not think what life would be without her."

Ishwar Dās was full of pity, but of sternness too. Perhaps Prabhū Dās felt only the sternness when the former said,—

"*Dare* not! That is not a word for a soldier of Christ. You can do *all* things through Christ—there is no exception—and believe me—I speak from experience—God never asks us to do impossibilities."

Then he told the story of his own life, and how all things had worked together for good.

The clock tower chimes rang out again and again, but the men did not hear them as they sat together in the high upper room and looked down on the city.

A white stream of moonlight flowed down the narrow street between the dark houses. Down it flitted the shadows of men carrying burdens, dark spots on the brightness; stray ghosts of the toilers of day they seemed, as no sound of their footsteps reached the onlookers from above. And so the time passed, until the moon, gliding towards the west, carried her light onwards, and the darkness, the true river of night, flowed on instead.

"One could sit for ever looking down upon this world of dreams," said Prabhū Dās.

"I fear it would not fit us for the world of reality, which, by the way, will soon dawn," answered his friend.

Prabhū Dās walked home by the quickening light ot the east, while his friend followed him with prayer and many anxious thoughts.

"God give him strength! otherwise to man this thing is impossible."

On the following evening, a few hours after her return from Rāmtīrath, Prabhū Dās told his wife how he had been led to become a Christian, and with shut eyes waited for a torrent of grief and reproach.

None came.

Looking up, he saw that her eyes were wet.

"God is good," she said simply.

CHAPTER IX

IF the news of Chandkor's death had reached him, Deviditta would have been unmoved, for, personally, his daughter was nothing to him; but when he heard that she had become a Christian, his grief and anger were great. For two days he could not eat, a circumstance that alarmed his wife, because abstinence was not habitual to him, nor could he sleep at night; but on the third day he was his calm, comfortable, torpid self again. "She is dead to us," he said, and that finished one episode of their life.

She was in fact worse than dead to them, because they never spoke of her again. Her memory and name were gone more completely than if the handfuls of dust, from her cremated body, had been thrown in the Ganges.

"Don't go to Deviditta's house," said Kishen Dei to Miss Gray about a week after the event. "They won't let you in, and they may say very wicked things to you."

The sight of one of the accursed nation would have been like a red rag to a bull at that time, so Miss Gray followed her old friend's advice.

Bibi Kishen Dei was sewing a jacket of home-made cotton cloth with a large needle, and untwisted cotton thread also of home manufacture. The pattern was simple in the extreme, and her stitches were of the largest, and when occasion required it, she hacked the material into shape with a sickle.

"I have got no scissors," she said in answer to Miss Gray's inquiring look, and with the conservative air of an old lady

who despises new-fashioned notions, she seized the sickle between her toes and sawed the cloth asunder.

"It serves him right," continued Kishen Dei. "Devidittā is
a villain. I could not wish him a worse punishment than this,
that a child of his should throw away her birth."

"She is born into the kingdom of God. Surely that is
worth the loss of all human privileges."

Kishen Dei shook her head. "You must think according to
your persuasion," she said ; "but that does not alter the fact
that Devidittā is a villain, and that he has been punished.
Yes, a villain," she went on, pricking the cloth viciously with
her needle as if each stitch were a stab into Devidittā's body.
"The large garden of mango trees about a mile from the
village belongs to him, and every one knows how he came by
it. Thieving and treachery! And there is no escape from him,
for sooner or later we must all fall under his hand, for what
can a poor man do when he needs money? Ah! you cannot know how troubled I am!" Kishen Dei pressed her hand
on her weather-beaten face as if to shut out the world.
"Can you interpret dreams, Miss Sahib? No? I have had
an awful dream, the same dream three times over towards
the dawn, and it is said that such dreams come true. Desolation is coming fast—I know it by all the visions I see--and
no one can prevent it. Nihāl Singh is a donkey, and Santo's
father is guileless as a babe. Gulāb Singh is far away, and
what can *I*, a poor old woman, do? I know of a woman who
fought against the angel of death and won. The angel had
come very often, and so knew the way to her house too well ;
so she blocked her door and opened another on the farther
side. He did not come again. But trouble comes in the
air and flows through the walls, and some troubles are worse
than death. No! you cannot help me, Miss Sahiba, *dear*
Miss Sahiba ; but it comforts old Kishani to let the smoke of
her heavy heart escape into your ear."

" I could not bear my troubles alone, Māī Kishandei ! "

"You! But you have no troubles ! You have no work to do, no cooking, no spinning, no exasperating children to weary you ! Why, Santo, Wanto, Durgi, Nāmo, and Jassa, with their perpetual '*chin-chin*' like sparrows, nearly send me mad at times ! To admonish them is useless ; one might as well try to reason with a crew of cats ! "

Bibi Kishen Dei quite brightened up as the details of her maternal and grandmotherly woes rose into her mind.

" But I have troubles too. Other people's children to look after, for instance—— "

" Ah, poor thing ! Still, you have so many alleviations—a servant to cook your bread, a doolie to ride in, beautiful clothes. By the way, will Chandkor dress as you do, and go about in a doolie, and eat beef, now that she has become a Christian ? "

"Christianity does not consist in eating and drinking, nor in clothing."

Kishen Dei was surprised.

" I thought you made Hindus into Christians by feeding them on beef, and Mohammedans Christians by giving them swine's flesh."

" No human power can make a Christian ; it is the work of God, who gives a new heart. Chandkor will probably eat and dress as she has always done."

Kishen Dei was lost in thought—but of other things, as her next question showed.

" Can you write a letter to the Deputy Commissioner about Khazān Singh ? You know he has eaten of the Government's salt by reading all its learning, and now he is ready to be a *tahsildār*. That would end all our troubles, because then he could help us."

She looked wistfully at Miss Gray.

"Could you ? "

E

It seemed hard to refuse, and it was a long while before Kishen Dei could understand that there was a still better way of approach to the "powers that be." But when Khazān Singh did eventually receive a smaller, though still coveted, office, and became in his mother's eyes a probable future re-storer of the family fortunes after many years, Kishen Dei attributed his success to Miss Gray's influence !

"British women have the art of getting their own way," she confided to a friend ; "even the men obey them ! "

Bibi Bhāg Dei had gone to the well with her husband's mid-day meal, and was coming wearily home again, when Miss Gray met her.

"No, I am not ill, only tired," she said with a very patient smile upon her impatient child, who beat her arm and protested against any stopping by the way.

"Jassa is much too heavy for you to carry ; he ought to walk, Bhāg Dei."

Miss Gray looked at him with all the maiden lady's ex-pression of disapproval in her eyes, which Jassa was quick to see. He returned the look with interest, accompanied with renewed kicks and howls.

"Hush ! hush ! my heart's ruby ! Don't cry. Look at the pretty flower."

But Jassa refused to be comforted. When, however, they all sat down, and he had the tinselled mirror off his mother's thumb ring, a door key, and a brass dish to do what he liked with, he condescended to sit in the dust and extract as much pleasure as he could from them—in noise.

"I shall never see Chandkor again, and my heart is sad. I liked her voice and her beautiful face. She taught me as much as she could ; but I am very stupid, and so I shall for-get it all."

"You cannot forget the hymn, Bibi—

'Come, Lord Jesus ! Dear Lord, come quickly;
Why tarriest Thou ? ' "

Jassa stopped to listen, and there was no sound nearer than
the lark's note above and the rustle of the breeze around them,
which swept the bearded barley into shining and shadow, like
the waves of a green sea.

"No, I shall always remember it for the love of you and
Chandkor."

"The Lord Himself loves you better still."

"I don't quite know, I am so stupid, and not used to love.
No one loved me till you and Chandkor did. You see, I have
always been one too many, always. My mother had five girls
one after the other. I was the fifth."

She checked each off on her fingers with a pathetic accuracy.

"The first was called Harnāmo, a nice name, because they
hoped she would be the last. The next was Rajī (satisfied),
they had had enough. The third Akhī (tired), because they
were weary of girls. The fourth Kaurī (bitter). I came fifth,
and when my mother saw me she said, ' Mar jā' (*i.e.* die !). So
I was called *Maro*."

The depressed life of the "one too many" had set its in-
delible brand on her poor face; the new name of Bhāg Dei,
given her by her husband's family, had presumably come too
late to alter her fortune.

"Your mother-in-law loves you too."

"Yes, she must do so, for she very seldom scolds me. I
can make very good bread, you see."

That, indeed, was her one virtue in the eyes of the family.

"A good quiet creature who can spin and cook and who
does what I tell her," was Kishen Dei's verdict when the new
daughter-in-law settled down to the routine of her husband's
home. A daughter-in-law may think herself fortunate who
has won such an opinion from her mother-in-law.

"Tell me, is she happy?" Bhāg Dei's thoughts had flown back to Chandkor.

"Yes, very happy."

"Is it very difficult to become a Christian?"

"Does Jassa find it very difficult to walk home?"   .

"I carry him."

"The Lord Jesus carries the lambs who can't walk in His arms. He can carry you, Bhāg Dei."

"He carries the stupid people who can't read in His arms?" said Bhāg Dei.

"Yes."

"I have been thinking so much about it, and wondering what would become of me. Chandkor is so clever, she could easily learn, and I am so stupid ; but if the Lord Jesus carries me across, it is all right."

Miss Gray said nothing. Bhāg Dei had been in a higher school already, for "none teacheth like Him."

"But what shall I do if—if I become a Christian? I *cannot* leave my children. I am not brave like Chandkor."

Bhāg Dei looked imploringly at her teacher.

"The Lord will be with you all the time, dear; don't be afraid. In the meanwhile, learn more of Him and pray to Him for grace for the time of need."

The Lord carried her safely unto the end, over all difficulties, in a still better way than either Bhāg Dei or her friend could have dreamed.

CHAPTER X

IT was about two o'clock in an afternoon of the month of June. A gentle, south-east wind caused a yellow haze to oppress the atmosphere. The gasping crows sat in the leafiest covert they could find, with beaks wide open. Even the chattering myna birds were still. The mangy dogs lay in the runnels where water had flowed from the village well that morning, for a slight suspicion of dampness still remained to cool their parched sides.

"The village seems asleep or dead," Bholā Singh muttered as he crept over to Deviditta's shop, "and that is just what I wanted. It would not do for Dittū Shāh to see me. His nickname is Kūhrā, the liar, and we all know how he deserves it." He had no difficulty in finding Deviditta, for the appointment to come and see the latter on business had been quietly made two days before as they passed casually in the street, and Deviditta had guessed what was coming. Deviditta was all smiles as he spread a rug for Bholā Singh's seat in the inner shop.

"What a great pity it is, Khālsājī, that you gentlemen never smoke. Your Guru was, no doubt, a most holy being, and must have had the best of reasons for forbidding it, but I confess, when my clients don't pay up, I do find it a great solace to gurgle my little hookah pipe. I wish I might have offered you a pipe, but, of course, I can't."

"No, Shāhjī," was the answer, "I cannot; but pray don't deny yourself at this time. Of course, we Sikhs cannot even smell a hookah pipe, but do you by all means smoke."

"Oh, no, Khālsājī; I could not think of being so unpleasant to you."

Bholā Singh began: "Well, Shāhjī, the truth is that I am quite tired of that Kūhrā. I owe him a matter of Rs. 150, but, do you know, he has added interest to principal, and charged compound interest on that, till he makes it out to come to Rs. 500, and threatens me with a lawsuit if I don't pay at once? I can't do it."

"Really," replied Deviditṭā, with true pain, "that is not at all handsome of him."

"Ah, is it, Shāhjī? And I such a good customer!"

"Very true, dear sir."

"Well, I wonder if you could help me by paying, say, Rs. 250 cash to him on my account, and I would then close all dealings with him, and deal only with you for ever after. We all know you to be a man of honour."

Pecksniff replied, "Well, Bhagwān knows that we are all sinners, but I do try to be as trusty as my late dear father was. He has become an inhabitant of heaven, as we know; his soul has mingled with the divine essence as a drop of water mingles with the rest of the liquid in the bucket, but his kindly admonitions to me will never, never fade from my mind." Much more of this passed, till it was agreed that if Dittū Shāh, the kūhrā, could be induced to accept Rs. 250 in hard cash, and give a stamped receipt in full quittance of all demands, the fly should be transferred from the web of a small spider to that of a large one in two days' time.

Ce n'est que le premier pas qui coute. "Now, dear friend," said the fly, "there is, unfortunately, another little matter. You know I have two marriageable daughters and a grand-daughter."

"Yes, Khālsājī, I know it. I have often wondered why you did not marry them off."

"Why (the farmer waxed a trifle warm), why? surely you

know that I am a poor man? Money cannot be picked up from the ground, and these three weddings would cost me Rs. 400, and even then I should be obliged to do everything more economically than that miserable cur, my cousin, Jīwan Singh."

"Oh, Singhji," was the answer, "of course, you must excel Jīwan Singh in all your arrangements. He *is* a poor creature. You can't afford to do it in the cheap and nasty style that he might adopt. Still I think that for *another* Rs. 100 you would outshine him as the sun outshines the moon. I tell you what, if you will give me a bond for Rs. 850 I'll pay your debt to Kūhrā, and provide all the needful expenses for all three girls whenever you want them."

"Oh, you are too kind. Do you really mean it?"

"Of course I do."

"But if I make a bond it will bear interest from the day I sign it, but I shan't want all the marriage expenses for six months yet."

"Well, of course, business is business, but then just think what advantages this plan will give you. First, you are for ever and ever set free from the vampire Kūhrā, who has sucked your blood for twenty years. Second, your three marriages will be the talk of the whole country-side as long as you live. Third, Jīwan Singh's liver will liquefy with vexation and shame at your success and renown. Fourth, my cashbox is placed at your disposal. You want Rs. 5 for the barber when he travels out to find bridegrooms for your girls? You have nothing to pay; I give it him. Your house folk want Rs. 50 for the wedding dresses? Just send in the bill to me. The firework maker asks for his little account. All he has to do is to give *me* a receipt for it, and he goes away joyful. You want a good milch buffalo for your daughter's dowry? Well, we are old friends. You know mine. She is really worth four score, but you can have her for absolutely nothing. I'll just write down three score against your name by way of remembrance that you took her; and if you like to take the calf, which is expected in a fortnight, why, it shall be yours too for a song. You never saw milk so rich and so plenteous as that buffalo gives. She is the sleekest of the herd which daily leaves this village. And when she goes into the house of your eldest daughter, whose gait is that of a goose, and whose eyes are those of a fawn, whose locks are like night, and whose face is the full moon shining through it, why, they will suit each other, as the jewel and its setting."

The fly had meanwhile, after the manner of flies, sucked a brown sweet which he had produced from his girdle. The fumes of the opium ball had by this time reached his poor addled brain, and a torpid excitement had paralyzed his sense of proportion. Half asleep, and wholly stupid, he left, after agreeing to everything; he left with a boa-constrictor's coil around his whole moral frame. The next day Deviditta beckoned him in, and told him that Dittū Shāh had agreed, not indeed for Rs. 250, but for Rs. 300, to let the debt be squared. In truth, Dittū Shāh had agreed to let Deviditta take Rs. 25 fee, and to receive the same sum himself as hush-money for saying nothing about it. The prize was caught. The Rs. 275 was paid to Dittū, and the wretched Bholā Singh was poorer by the Rs. 50 as the first step on his downward road.

CHAPTER XI

ALTHOUGH Sikh priests are called upon to perform ceremonies by the orthodox, the Jat Sikhs, in many religious matters, are practically Hindus ; so Bholā Singh, instead of following the precepts of the Granth, went to consult the Brahman Prohit, or priest, about the weddings of Santo, Wanto, and Durgi.

The Prohit consulted the stars of the respective brides and bridegrooms, and then fixed the lucky time. It was a fortunate coincidence that the heavenly bodies allowed the triple wedding to take place on the same day. But previous to this many arrangements had taken place, involving both care and thought, as the following facts regarding a Hindu marriage will show. First of all the husband must be procured ; secondly comes the ceremony of the engagement ; lastly the wedding feast. Both the trouble and the expense of it all fall upon the bride's parents. It is their business to find a husband. The barber, as a faithful family servant—an Eliezer of Damascus, in fact—is the match-maker. He goes round the neighbouring villages in search of an eligible " parti," and brings back word. If the girl's parents approve of the young man and his family, they send back the barber with the proposal. " Eliezer " takes with him a few rupees, some dates and cocoanut, and a red and white cotton skein, called *māuli*, which, if the proposal is accepted, he puts into the hands of the bridegroom-elect in the presence of friends. The ceremony of the engagement then begins ; it is performed by the Prohit. When the lucky day arrives the wedding takes place at the house of the bride's father. The wedding party, consisting of the bridegroom, with his parents, relations, and friends, arrives in the evening and departs the next morning ; but its stay is sometimes prolonged for a day or two if the bride's parents can afford it, and so desire it. The night is spent in feasting and music, and ends in the tying of the marriage knot : no metaphor in this case, as the skirts of the bride and bridegroom are tied together. After this they march three times round a fire. The bride goes to her father-in-law's house after the wedding feast. As a rule she stays there for three days, and then returns to her own parents. When she is old enough the *muklāwa*, or final ceremonies, are performed, after which she and her husband live with the rest of the family in his father's house. This rule is not observed when the bride is a grown-up young woman, or if the parents are not well off. In either case the *shādi*—wedding—and *muklāwa*—marriage ceremonies—are gone through at the same time.

All this costs time and money, but the most important and certainly the most expensive item is the feast. For days it has been preparing ; cauldrons of ghi, and sugar, and rice, have been converted into sweetmeats, and cakes, and savoury dishes, in strange contrast to the usual frugal manner of living. The bride's relations and friends of the village, as well as the bridegroom's party, are invited to partake, which they do, ladies and gentlemen apart. The menials, that is, water-carriers, washermen, minstrels, barbers, potters, carpenters, smiths, and sweepers, are fed separately from a large heap spread on a cloth on the ground. This is called *Khurli-pāna*—manger-feeding—*i.e.*, as the cattle are fed. But let it not be supposed that they eat together ! There are as many grades amongst the so-called menials as amongst their employers, and each holds aloof from the sweeper, the lowest

A TOFFEE AND HIS APPRENTICE.

Showing the wheel, and hundreds of freshly made lamps.

and the least—the outcaste, in fact, who has neither name nor place amongst them. They are fed, in varying quantities, according to rank, the amount given depending upon the family income. Added to this is a sum of money. Seven being a lucky number, it is given in sevens of copper or silver, according to wealth. The barber, in his capacity of match-maker, gets the lion's share. All the remains of the feast fall to him, as nothing must be kept by the family. He usually sells it to the sweetmeat makers, and often makes a good profit. Money is also thrown amongst the crowd, sometimes silver, but more often the thick, old-fashioned coins called *Nānak shāhi paisa*, which are kept for this purpose. This last custom, however, is discouraged by Government, whose desire is to check the reckless extravagance which characterizes all Indian weddings.

All this was a sore trial to Kishen Dei's frugal mind, but it could not be helped; the family honour, the desire of eclipsing Jīwan Singh, and the custom of ages demanded it. But she did what she could to keep expenditure within certain limits. The feast lasted but one night, the *shādi* and *muklāwa* ceremonies were observed at the same time, and the largess was brown instead of white.

Bholā Singh had brought to her a quantity of silver coins in his trembling hands. She took it quietly without remonstrance (to the good man's relief), and as quietly locked it up, putting a mass of coppers in the bag instead.

What a hot night it was, and how the drums beat! But the three little brides in red felt no inconvenience. It was delightful to sit in beautiful clothes with nothing to do, but allow themselves to be admired, and to feel—a rare sensation —that they could not be done without. Santo and Wanto, the unready and unwished for, were both vain and uplifted during these giddy hours of prosperity.

It was a starry night, and a young moon lay low in the west, and Sleep looked down upon the village, but the bright lights and songs drove him away. No one desired his presence, save a few sick folk, and all the babies into whose wide-open, unwinking eyes fell a few flakes of down from his soft wings as he flew away.

Bhāg Dei, with the soundly sleeping Jassa in her arms, and Jassi snoring beside her, did her part as bride's mother with the quiet patience which characterized her. All unconsciously she did the "next thing," whether it was cooking or spinning or a more rare social duty, with the humble grace of the woman who did "what she could." But her heart was with Durgi, who at the dawn would leave her. All the childish faults were forgotten, all the times, when sorely tried, she had told her to get out of her way. She remembered them only as a cause for pitying love. Would the mother-in-law bear with these girlish moods that try even a mother's love to the utmost? She looked at her; the face was hard, there were very evident lines of it, although she was listening in smiling politeness to Kishen Dei.

"She will do justly by her, I am sure of that, but will she *love mercy* ? "

It is well for us that our questions are left for the years to answer.

The bridegrooms meanwhile were looking shy and uncomfortable amongst the men. They had not the feminine capacity of getting pleasure from their dress ; the saffron-coloured garment with the covering of tinsel and flowers was rather a source of discomfort. Perhaps the only part of the ceremony they enjoyed was the good things so liberally given them to eat. Neither bride nor bridegroom could be supposed to have any interest in each other, being not only strangers, but at an age when childhood's toys are more appreciated than the graver duties of life.

The stars faded one by one, the far hills lay in a violet line against the east, and the new day began.

With the sun came the preparations for departure : the bridegrooms mounted with their fathers on horses painted in red and blue checks for the occasion; each little animal trotting off gaily with its two riders into the plain willingly, because its face was towards its own stables.

Litters covered with red awaited the brides, but their movements were not so rapid owing to the lengthy leave-takings. They were embraced and wept over by all their aunts and cousins, and last of all by their mothers. Santo and Wanto tried to cry, because it was expected of them, but it is not recorded whether they succeeded in the attempt. But Durgi went away with a heavy heart, not because she feared the future, but because the bitter tears of her mother fell upon her like an unlooked-for storm of rain.

" Be good, Durgi, my love! Be good, and do whatever your *sās* (mother-in-law) wishes," she whispered brokenly as she looked within the curtains of the doolie for the last time. And Durgi, for the first time in her little life, began to think.

The doolies were carried at a swinging pace over the fields, and soon to Bhāg Dei's straining eyes they dwindled into three little red spots and disappeared.

" I am glad it is all over," said Kishen Dei.

CHAPTER XII

JUNE passed in burning heat, then came July, but no rain, so the wells creaked night and day, and the poor oxen had to do double work upon less food.

"The rain should come soon," said Bholā Singh the hopeful. "I saw the ants carrying their stores into shelter underground."

"If it doesn't Moti will die (Moti was one of the oxen). He grows thinner every day, and ought to have less work and more food, instead of which it is all the other way round."

Nihāl Singh looked gloomily at the animals as they ate their starving allowance by the dripping well-wheel which had ceased for the mid-day hours.

"I have to drag the poor thing up each time to be harnessed; he has no strength to rise. Every one knows that such a state of things can't go on for ever."

"Patience, my son; the Lord of the heavens is merciful, and the ants——"

"The ants know nothing about it; even if the rain comes to-night it may be too late."

A week passed and still no rain. The dust whitened the leaves of the parched trees by the roadside, the earth shrank and cracked under the burning of the heavens, but man and beast strove steadily to keep the crops alive, and each thing grew and ripened in its season.

At last heavy clouds gathered, and the longed-for rain fell, but only for a few hours. It was what the villagers call the first droppings, which freshen the earth, and fill the pools, a harbinger of the rains proper which flood the land, and sink down through the crust, till their waters reach the moisture beneath. Then, and not till then, is the thirsty land satisfied. Nothing short of weeks of moisture and mist and covering clouds could relieve the tension of the hot winds and the unveiled sun, and prepare the clods for the sowing of the winter's crop.

But what a change a few hours of rain can bring! All the hollows, hitherto dry and empty, had become ponds, in which the children were swimming gaily; the fields, even the waste places, looked green; little red, velvety, ground spiders were trotting about amongst the grass; and the frogs in brand-new yellow suits, soon to be browned by the sun, croaked in the ditches. Every living thing rejoiced except Moti the ox, which had lain down for the last time the night before.

A new animal was bought to fill the gap, but the old ox, faithful to his dead comrade, refused to be yoked with the stranger, so he had to be sold at a loss, and a new pair procured, involving Bholā Singh in further difficulties. His debt was now augmented by Rs. 95, and Deviditta rejoiced. He sat in his shop and made money with still less effort than heretofore, because his son, Gopāl Chand, a son after his own heart, did whatever active service came in the way.

It was now about the 23rd of July, and the long-delayed monsoon was ready to burst at last. The air was heavy with the coming storm, but Deviditta, seemingly impervious to all climatic impressions, was sitting calmly happy in the inner room of the shop. Things had gone well with him, field being added to field, and wealth flowed in. Was there no one to tell him that a woe was coming on the wings of the blast? No doubt, apparently, troubled him. His mind

was full of pleasant thoughts, and he smiled from time to
time as he said,—

"Poor old Bholā! Poor fool!"

He had forgotten just then that his younger son, Motī Lāl,
was ill. Perhaps it was because he had not seen much of
him since Gopāl Chand had become his right hand in the
business. Motī Lāl was dreamy and unpractical, the darling
of his mother, and therefore did not hold a large place in
his father's heart or mind. But still he was a son, and now
and then anxious thoughts would cross his father's mind
about the fever which went on from day to day, and he
offered the *hakīm* a liberal reward if he would make the boy
well. The *hakīm* was a clever man, and acted according to
his lights, but he did not know that he had a case of typhoid
fever to deal with.

It was now the twenty-first day of its course, and the
mother, who had watched her son long, thought him better.
She said,—

"His mind is clearer, I think; he does not call so constantly for—Chandkor."

Deviditttā said nothing, and went to bed on the roof. The
allusion to Chandkor was unpleasant to him. That was a
reason why he so seldom went near the sick bed, the
constantly reiterated cry "Chandkor" being as gall and
wormwood.

"Chandkor was very good to me, mother. She comforted me whenever I was ill or in trouble, and her voice
follows me everywhere. Do you remember how she sang—

'Why tarriest Thou? Come, Lord Jesus'?"

"Hush, my son! You must throw these words far away—
into the well, anywhere!"

Bibi Kishen Dei looked terror-stricken.

Motī Lāl laughed—a low, trembling laugh.

"Oh, the well! The deep well whose waters gleam from the darkness, like the stars at night! How cool and quiet it would be there!"

"No! no! Speak not of it, my son! Sleep! See! your mother will put you to sleep as she used to do when you were a little child."

"Yes, mother, I am going to sleep. I feel better now; and do you sleep too, and Gopāl," he added, with a rare thoughtfulness.

And they slept, the tired mother on a bed near her son, and Gopāl by his father on the roof, while the air was hot and stifling with the gathering storm.

Deviditţā slept heavily, and moaned in his sleep, for he was wrapped in the folds of a dream.

He seemed to be standing at his door while a crowd of people pressed round him. They were of the large company of the disappointed, those in debt, and bitter of soul, and had come to him for help. It was in vain, for he had none to give. Lastly, Bholā Singh, laying his head in the dust, pleaded as a captive does for life.

Deviditţā put his foot on the old man's neck, and—the ghostly crowd faded away. The pipal tree in the wall shivered, the crack widened, and with a crash his dwelling lay around him in heaps of sand.

"Father! Father!" Gopāl Chand shook the bed violently. "Father!"

The thunder crashed overhead, and gleams of lightning made spaces of day in the night.

"Ah! What a dream! I am glad you woke me, Gopāl. The very devils of hell had hold of me."

"Father! we can't find Motī Lāl."

Deviditţā, still stupefied with sleep, followed Gopāl with difficulty down the steep steps, so slippery with the rain.

Bibi Kishen Dei was weeping bitterly in the court, the centre

F

of a wondering group of servants and neighbours, who had come to see what had happened.

The news of trouble flies on eagles' wings. A search party went out with lanterns, regardless of wind and rain, but nothing was found till the morning. When the water-carrier went to the well, he saw something white in the dark depth. It was Moti Lāl.

In an access of delirium he had run out while all were asleep, and whether he stumbled over the edge of the well, which was at the end of the outer court, with no protecting wall round it, or whether in a mad desire for water he had attempted to draw the rope, no one knew.

Deviditta felt as much grief as he was capable of, but time, and prosperity, and his remaining son, brought comfort. As far as outsiders could judge, he was unchanged, and the routine of buying and selling, of oppression and treachery, went on as before, until—the end came, for because of all this the hand of the great Nemesis was stretched out still.

SIKH PEASANTS.

Attending District Magistrate's Court on circuit.

CHAPTER XIII

THE visit of a Government official is not an unmixed pleasure to the people. As it is a State affair, it involves a certain amount of expense, and so brings terror to the good as well as to the evil-doer!

And it is unavoidable.

The ruler himself may be humane and of the simplest habits, but he brings with him an *entourage* which demands in his name service both of body and estate from the villagers, because the "Barā Sāhib" must have everything, and because his servants must gain as much as they can.

The people of Maure, therefore, from the least to the greatest, were much perturbed when a Government messenger announced that the district magistrate intended to encamp on the plain in a few days.

A committee of chiefs sat on the great wooden seat at the door of the head man's house, and discussed the matter gravely for some hours, amid the sounds of the barking of village dogs and lowing of village kine. Contributions of grain, fodder, and bedding for the horses, and milk and fowls for the Sahib's *ménage*, were levied and arranged for; also a contingent of sweepers to watch the camp during the night.

On the third day the news of the arrival of the baggage camels reached the ears of the youth of the place, who immediately departed for the scene of action. So the unloading took place in the presence of all the rising generation without

exception—not even a baby was left behind! The tent-
pitchers and other servants were watched with the deepest
interest, and a detailed account was carried home with the
accuracy of reporters of the Press.

Kishen Dei was stripping the maize cobs with her strong
hand when Jassi ran in with Jassa in her arms, or, rather,
poised on her side, for Jassi, although not much bigger than
her charge, now reigned as nurse in the place of Durgi.

"I have seen such wonderful things!" she said breathlessly. "The white cloth houses—a whole street of them—
are standing on the waste ground. I saw them put up and
tied with rope. There are chairs and tables and boxes—*great*
boxes. What a rich man the 'Barā Sāhib' must be!"

"Is the 'mem' coming, too?"

"Yes, and two children."

"Then I'll go to see them," said Kishen Dei. "I did not
see half of what I wished to last time, because she was not
there."

Early next morning a lordly khānsāmān, or butler, entered the village. He was resplendent in a coat with brass
buttons; his girdle (which is, of course, worn round the waist
during service) was thrown jauntily over one shoulder, after
the manner of a gentleman at large. He also carried a cane
—another badge of gentility. It was like a royal progress
—the portly figure in front, Jassi and the baby, with about
fifty others of her class, following behind. The train stopped
at many doors, first at Deviditta's, where the khānsāmān
indulged in an hour's gossip about his master's concerns.
The dignitary aforesaid would have been surprised what an
amount of matter the proverbial bird of the air can carry
in his bill. The Sahib's income, his expenditure thereof—
followed by a judgment upon adequacy and proportion—his
temper, health, and family affairs, all trickled in little runnels
of information between the gurgles of the "huqqa" which the

butler shared with a maulvi, who joined the conclave by
common interest and attraction. Refreshed by social inter-
course, the *chef* then went to market with the laudable intention
of buying at a minimum, and subsequently selling at a
maximum cost to his mistress.

Bholā Singh met him with a screaming fowl in his arms.

"Take this, *sheikhjī*," he said with a childish eagerness.
"Cook it for the supper of the 'Barā Sāhib,' and tell him that
it is the gift of his servant Bholā Singh."

The khānsāmān took it with condescension, felt the creature, and ordered it to be sent to the camp. Mentally he
had decided how much he should charge for it in the account.
Aloud he assured Bholā that he would present it to the "Barā
Sāhib" as his gift.

"I think it is a good one," Bholā said anxiously. "I bought
it from the maulvi for the Sahib, so that he should remember
me."

"Have you remembered to give orders for the night
watch?"

"I have got six men ready, 'mahārāj.' They will watch
while the Presence sleeps."

The butler then proceeded to make his purchases of the
few odds and ends still wanting : the bulk of requirements
having been already procured in town, or from the grocers
and oilmen, who had been ordered to open temporary shops
at the camp.

On his way back to the camp, the *chef* stopped at the
little mosque in the Mohammedan quarter of the village, and,
taking off his shoes, went in to pray.

If not justified, he came out again none the less assured
of his acceptance before God.

The Sahib and his family arrived in the evening.

*   *   *   *   *   *

"Mother! *Mother! Do* come and look at this little girl and a *dear* little baby!"

No one heard apparently, so the intense young person oı nine years ran indoors.

"Oh, mother, *do* come! There is a funny old lady too, with rings on her toes, and a big ring in her nose!"

Mrs. —— was busy unpacking a few personal effects, but she came nevertheless, and was received by Kishen Dei with great gravity and dignity.

"Sit down, 'Mem Sahib,'" said the old Sikh lady, accustomed to command.

The "Mem Sahib" sat down, and, although she had very few words at her command, they were uttered with such grace that her visitors were charmed.

* * * * * *

"She is the most beautiful lady I ever saw, and so kind. I shall certainly call upon her again, and, if I can make her understand, perhaps I may induce her to plead with her husband for Khazān Singh. A word would do it. It would cost her nothing, and be everything to us."

This is a digest of a long conversation in the firelight by the Bholā Singh family, before the several members wrapped themselves in their quilts for the night.

But all the cold night through the watchers sat by the camp fire and smoked, striving to keep awake by pulls at the common pipe in their midst, and by tales of the hard day's work now over. So they watched and slept and smoked by turns till the *Muazzin* from the mosque called the Mohammedan world to prayer and the cock-crow brought in the dawn.

CHAPTER XIV

"HERE, Rose, Rose," shouted Devidittā as he reached the ample threshing-floor early one April morning, where all Bholā Singh's wheat harvest was stacked. "Rose, what are you about? Not awake yet?"

A sleepy voice replied, "Oh, shāhjī, don't be angry. I told Margaret to wake me, but he has gone off to give provender to his cow, whose calf was born yesterday; and Grace is still fast asleep there on the cot. As for Ruby, he is dog-tired with our winnowing all day yesterday.[1] We really stayed awake till dawn for fear of thieves and incendiaries, but we have committed a fault. Pray say nothing more about it."

"Ah, but I will. You know that, although this crop is called Bholā Singh's, it is really mine. It was I who put on you four young fellows, because I knew you to be stout and hearty. You know I have many enemies. What should I have done if Bholā Singh's angry uncle's son had come with a lucifer match at midnight and fired all these stacks? Ruby! Grace! Margaret!" he shouted as each sheepish youth arrived, "I'll put on an extra couple of rupees to all your accounts in my books as a fine for your carelessness."

By this time Bholā Singh had also arrived. He knew the crop was only his in name. He knew that after the weddings he had paid Rs. 123 in cash, and the produce of his best sugar-cane brake, which was worth a good Rs. 378, but which

---

[1] Gulāb, Motī, Fazl, and Lāl are extremely common names or men.

had only been credited as worth Rs. 234 in the usurer's
books.   He knew that his beautiful wheat crop, the pride of
the village, was really worth the full balance of the debt, but
that he should get but a fourth of its value allowed out of the
principal, and that, in fact, the original bond of Rs. 850 was
still standing at Rs. 635, though he had paid Rs. 1,000
worth of produce and cash towards it in these two sad years
since the weddings.   He knew all this.   But still he talked
big, and scolded Grace, Ruby, Margaret, and Rose as lustily
as did Deviditta for their unwatchfulness, as though it were
himself whom they had wronged.   However, now all were
busy again.   An angry sun, rapidly becoming hotter, had
roused a smart breeze.   Grace had yoked a pair of starveling
oxen to the bundle of brushwood which was being driven over
the prostrate corn-sheaves.   The grain was being separated,
and Rose had taken his stand with a wide winnowing-fan raised
high above his head to shake the contents gently down, and
allow the wind to sever the chaff from the golden grain, which
fell in an ever-increasing heap at his dusty feet.   A towering
mass of barley lay in one corner of the floor.   A tangled
hillock of vetches, with acid pods and round peas within them,
was stored in another.   But the strength of the party was
given to the precious wheat.   Deviditta had made a most
advantageous time bargain with Ralli Brothers, the great
London corn-factors, for delivery of twenty tons on the 1st of
May.   He was very anxious to secure his produce in good
time, so he sat by for the greater part of the hot day urging on
his slaves (as they had become through the operation of their
several debts) to work almost beyond endurance, till it was too
dark to see the chaff from the wheat.   He then sent one of
them to bring his bedstead from his house, a mile over the
fields, that he might lie there himself all night, and extract a
few more minutes' toil from them next morning than he had
secured this day.   Bholā Singh, dejected, barely able to

endure the rebukes of his spouse at the loss of all things, wended his listless way home at nightfall. Somehow he could not work as was his wont. Age was creeping over him. The future mortgage of all his land was looming before him. But for the present it was recorded in the Government registers as his own. He was still a landowner. A suck at the opium-ball refreshed and inspirited him, and he slept.

A month later. The threshing-floor is empty. Ralli Brothers have carried off all the wheat. The crop of vetches has gone into Deviditta's granary. Bholā Singh has received a half of the barley, and a cwt. of the wheat—one cwt. out of 400 !—as his supply for six months till the millet and maize may ripen in November. Till then he and his must live on the pittance the usurer may allow them. But the catastrophe was hastened. Nihāl Singh, the eldest son, went one afternoon to see a wrestling match. After it was over, he and his mates adjourned to the public-house. A bottle of the ardent spirit, distilled from the bark of the acacia and molasses, was handed round, followed by another, and another. On their return home the men suddenly met Deviditta. Nihāl Singh's wrath burst forth in vile abuse, such as cannot be here recorded.

The usurer savagely muttered, "Well, I can punish you for this, and I will. Let Bhagwān be witness."

Two days after he called on Bholā Singh. " Now, sir, you know your son filthily abused me two nights ago. I have had enough of it. You will be good enough to pay up, or write me a mortgage of all your land."

Entreaty, appeals to old friendship, abject apology, were all in vain. The penitent author of the trouble came, and with a gesture of the unspeakable humiliation incurred by baring his long Sikh locks, kneeled with his head in the dust at the usurer's feet, conjuring him to be merciful. "No ; a mortgage or a law-suit." The perils of the latter were too well known, and ten rupees were added to the account next day for the stamp paper on which the mortgage was to be engrossed. It was first drafted on a plain sheet, in these words : " Know all men, by these presents, that I, Bholā Singh, son of Kirpa Singh, Jat, clan Sandhū, inhabitant of the village of Maure, Tehsil Shikārpore, District Amritsar, being in debt to the amount of one thousand rupees (Rs. 1,000), the half of which is five hundred rupees (Rs. 500), to Lālā Devidittā Shāh, son of Lālā Disaundha Rām, caste Arorā, of the same village, do hereby mortgage to the said Lālā Devidittā Shāh the whole of my arable lands in the said village, numbered in the Government registers as follows : Nos. 65, 66, 67, 189, half of 245, three-fourths of 263—in all, acres 67, roods 3, poles 5—and do hereby give possession of the same to the said mortgagee, to have and enjoy the produce of the same, setting off the same against the said debt and interest at one rupee per cent. per mensem. Provided that I, the mortgagor, shall have the option at any time of re-entering on the land by paying up the balance of the said debt with interest at the above rate. In witness whereof, etc., etc., etc. Dated 16 Hār, in the year 1980, Vikramājīt era."

The next day a procession set out from Maure. First rode the money-lender, on a lanky pony whose tail was three and a half feet in length, bearing the deed in his pocket. At a long distance followed Bholā Singh, on a starveling pony of a quarter the value of the one ahead, whose one brown and one pink eye looked forth mournfully from its unkempt face-locks. There was the labourer Rose, to hold them on arrival at their destination ; and a kind friend of Bholā's, one Amīr Singh, who accompanied him to bear him up in all that lay before him that sad day. They sauntered along the paths for some miles, and finally turned into the same broad highway along which the five gay recruits had merrily walked two short years before. Reaching the registry office in the heart of the city, the deed was taken by Devidittā to the registering clerk, a friend of his own, through whose civility it was copied soon and entered in the book and laid before the honest Englishman whose signature was required. He scrutinized the varying countenances of the group before him, and incredulously asked Bholā, "Have you really received all this large sum of money?"

"Yes, my lord."

"Do you really, of your own free will, mortgage the whole of your ancestral lands to a stranger like this?"

"Yes, my lord."

There was no help for it. With a sigh of unbelief the officer affixed his name, and the deed was handed back to the creditor, now no longer the waste paper which it had been till that moment, but converted into a scourge, nay, rather a sword, which should devour—but whom? The debtor or the creditor? Events will show.

The fee for copying and registration was six and a half rupees. Ere the party left the city, they all sat down under the shade of the Small Cause Court, and an account-book was produced by the banker. A new page was turned over, and a scratch made at the head to indicate the trunk of the elephant-god Ganesh, whose protection is implored at the outset of every undertaking. The entry on a new house, the setting forth on a burglary, the commencement of a pilgrimage to atone for the sins of that burglary and all else, the opening of a new ledger of fraud or faith, all must be put under the tutelage of Srī Srī Ganesh. This having been done, the six and a half rupees were gravely entered, as the first item in the new account, and the pen was handed to Bholā Singh to touch, in token that he accepted the entry as correct. The first link in the second fetter was forged. The well-fed brown pony, which had had a good feed of corn during the halt at the expense of a client whom Bholā Singh had spied on arrival, was quite ready to amble gaily home. The starveling, which had wistfully eyed his luckier comrade enjoying himself all the while that Rose had held one with his right hand and one with his left, was in no such fettle, and he and his load reached Maure two hours after the banker.   Old Kishen Dei saw both of them arrive.   She knew that her old husband and his stalwart sons were henceforth but serfs on their ancestral lands, and that it was now night.

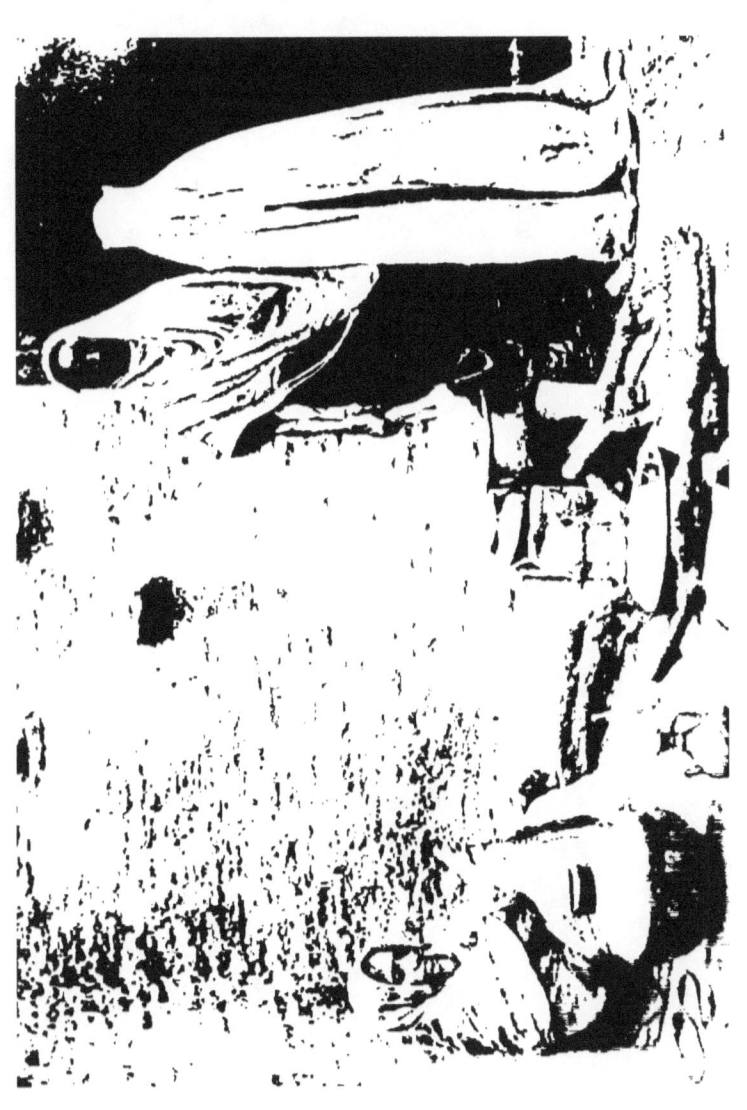

CHAPTER XV

LIFE in the East is simple as a word that a child may read, but it is an Eastern word which spells backwards. The present points ever to the past; the work of the day down to its commonest detail bears the stamp of history. That woman who uncoils the length of rope " to draw with because the well is deep "; the weaver at the loom; the blind beggar by the wayside; Lazarus at the gate; the widow mourning for her son—all work and wait and suffer as they did when the healing hem of the Master's garment swept through the wheat-fields of Galilee.

It was still early in the morning, but the temperature had risen considerably, when Miss Gray reached Maure after a year's absence. She had seen the rapid swing of time and change in the West, had found a new sphere of work in another part of India on her return, made new friends—and now, coming back to the old district, was surprised to find it as it had always been. No change apparently had visited the place—the pond; the tree; the mud walls, over which familiar faces greeted her with a kindly welcome; the very dust heaps seemed the same. The year had passed away like a watch in the night.

She passed the outskirts of the village, where all the rags and bones and odds and ends are thrown; by the square platform of earth where the potter works, thankful for the little patches of shade which the stunted acacia throws upon him;

by the outer wall, reeking with heat, where the weaver's womankind walk backwards and forwards for thirty yards unwinding the thread from the distaff on to stakes fastened in the ground ; past open doorways through which came the hum of the spinning-wheel, until she entered the village, where the higher walls cast a dark shade—not a shade of coolness, but a purple depth of colour.

She stood for a minute to look at the well-known scene, and her thoughts, which had gone forward and outward, crept backwards as the shadow on the dial of Ahaz. It was no interruption, but rather a continuance of her dream, when a woman stopped in front of her and said :

"She whom thou lovest is sick ! "

It was Arūrī, the sweeper woman, who used to grind corn at Bholā Singh's door. She was on her way thither at the time.

" Bhāg Dei is very ill ; she has been ill for a long time, but you have never come to see her."

She asked many questions about the wonderful journey across the sea as they walked together. It was a keen pleasure, something akin to new life, to talk to one who did not despise her—the sweeper whose clothing was dusty and worn, and who was called by a name which meant muck and mire.

Kishen Dei was working as usual, and harder than ever now that there was no patient daughter-in-law to cook and spin ; but she did not plead lack of time to see her friend.

"Where have you been all these months ? And why have you not come to see us ? Have you forgotten your old friend now that her troubles have come and settled down like the locusts upon the green leaves? *Not* forgotten ! Ah well ! sit down. You have twisted my 'takla' I see ! "

(Miss Gray's dress had caught in the needle, which indeed was not surprising, as several spinning-wheels were on end, each with a sharp spike projecting as if seeking injury.)

"But never mind! *Oh jāne* (let alone). Kishen Dei has heavier griefs to bear than a twisted needle. Loss of every-thing—very little wheat to grind now—ask Arūrī! And now I must cook as well, for you see Bhāg Dei is ill. It is now night for me, but you come like the moon. Nay, wait a while, you shall see Bhāg Dei presently. Comfort your old friend first. My heart has become cool by your presence."

It was no easy matter to follow Kishen Dei's incoherent story, interrupted from time to time by expressions of affection, and inquiries about England.

"Did you see the Queen? No! Why not? Was she too busy to send for you? I had hoped that you would call upon her and tell her that Gulāb Singh works for her in Africa."

Kishen Dei scarcely recovered from this disappointment! To her, the Queen was a great chieftainess who sat on a large bed, in a magnificent courtyard, and listened to the tales of woe or need of whoever came.

"And tell me, how did you reach England? do you go by train or *ekka* (gig)?"

"It is many miles over the sea, Bibi. I went in a ship."

Kishen Dei called to remembrance the ferry-boat in which she had crossed the Rāvī when she married and left her "country" and father's house. "A man stands at one end and steers with a pole, does he not? No! Then how does the thing move?"

Miss Gray tried to explain the breadth and depth of the Indian Ocean, but as she had nothing at hand but the village pond wherewith to liken it, she gave it up. She had moreover no wish to prolong the conversation, as her heart was with the silent heap on the bed at the other end of the yard.

"Yes, you may go," said Kishen Dei at last, reluctantly. "Go and see if you can make her well. It is so difficult for me to cook as well as do all the work of the house."

Bhāg Dei was very ill. Miss Gray did what she could, and

told Kishen Dei how to give the medicine, which she hoped to send in a few hours; then she tried to say a few words, but the weary eyes had no answering look in them.

"She does not know me!"

"She doesn't know her children, so I make them play all day at the well. You see *I* have no time to look after them," said Kishen Dei.

Two days brought little change apparently, but on the third Bhāg Dei had reached the Borderland.

Miss Gray knelt beside the bed and felt the flickering pulse. She knew that nothing more could be done, but asked Kishen Dei to bring a hot brick for the icy feet. It seemed strange that even death could bring a chill when the rays of the sun were as fire. Mortal weakness was upon her, but she was conscious. When Miss Gray spoke to her she smiled. Some of her relations had come, hearing that she was dying, but they had gone out for a while; the children were playing outside, so she lay in peace—great peace, Miss Gray thought. Then she seemed to say something which, although she bent her head to listen, Miss Gray failed to understand. Thinking that perhaps it was a request for a hymn, the invariable request of old days, she sang very softly a few lines of the well-known hymn :—

> " Come, Lord Jesus, come quickly ;
> Why tarriest Thou ? "

The lips moved again, and this time the words, although low, were clear :—

> " Lord Jesus, come. "

And the Lord tarried not His coming, for even while they were speaking of Him He came.

*　　*　　*　　*　　*　　*

Bhāg Dei lay in great peace, while the musicians sang and her relations wailed around her.

The problem of life, which she could not solve, had been·
taken out of her hands.

A while after the dead was laid on a framework of wood,
and carried by six bearers, three on each side, to the Marghat or place of cremation.

The musicians went in front singing :—

"Sat nām sat hai"
(The true name of God is the only true) ;

while those behind answered :—

" Harkā nām sat hai "
(The name of God is true).

The sentence was in cadence, and the sound rose and fell
to the steady tread of the bearers in mournful unison.

When they reached the Marghat the body was laid on
piled-up fuel. The nearest relatives lit the pile on each side,
and the cleansing fires soon covered it from sight.

The red grave smouldered all night, and in the morning
a few handfuls of ashes were taken away, to be kept in an
urn until they could be thrown into the Ganges. A hillock
of mud was all that remained to mark the place.

But precious in the sight of the Lord is the death of His
saints, so the little mound with neither name nor date was
none the less a quiet sleeping-place for one of His tired
pilgrims, for a little while, until He come.

CHAPTER XVI

A LL lusts grow by that which they feed upon, the lust of gold particularly. Hence it arose that Devidittā grieved at not yet having become owner of the fair lands of Bholā Singh, being still but a mortgagee. He resolved to cure this defect, and took an early opportunity, after the events narrated in the last few chapters, to remind his victim of the great outlay which he had incurred on the weddings of the three girls, and on the mortgage of the land. In vain the debtor pleaded that at any rate the mortgage was an accomplished fact, that ever since its execution Devidittā had taken all the produce, leaving a miserable pittance for the family support. The only answer was an invitation to come over and see how the account stood, at an early hour the next day. When the downcast father and son seated themselves on the dusty bit of sacking which lay on the high step at the shop front, the ponderous books were brought out. The leaves, each three feet long and six inches broad, were slowly turned over till the account was reached, and the total of the debt was stated to be Rs. 1,833. " But, shāhjī," feebly murmured the late landowner, " the bond was only for Rs. 850. I paid you large sums, and yet you forced me to execute a possessory mortgage for Rs. 1,000, and ever since then you have had the whole of the produce. There must surely be a mistake somewhere."

" No, indeed ; I have not learnt arithmetic for nothing. I

can assure you your memory is at fault. The debt now comes to Rs. 1,833."

This bare-faced demand roused the Sikh fire in the old man's breast. He jumped down into the street. "Let the Gurūji judge between us. I will not pay."

Shylock deliberately folded up his long pages, tied the red leather cover neatly round with the greasy twine attached to it, tucked the end of the said twine into the bend, and put the book into his safe, which was merely a hole sunk in the dry ground and secured by a trap-door. He then calmly considered how much more he could manage to add to the account before the following Tuesday, when it would be lucky to institute an action against Bholā Singh in the Civil Court. Tuesday turned out wet. The journey was therefore deferred till the next lucky day, which was Saturday. He reflected that, all Saturdays and Tuesdays being lucky days, the scriveners who engross plaints are very busy. He therefore started before dawn, and reached the precincts of the Court-house by 8 a.m.

A writer was there who combined with a facile pen a long acquaintance with the methods of dusting the Court's eyes. Soon Deviditta was pouring out his troubles into his sympathizing breast. After a careful inspection of the account the writer said, "I think, my brother, that you might very well open two accounts. You see that if you have only one it will be easy for the defendant to prove the payments of so much wheat, so much cane-juice, so much cotton, so much millet, so much vetches. The village lands have been all lately surveyed, and the yield of all is pretty well known to the Government officials. Your village accountant is an honest man, anxious to stand well with his superiors; he will probably be not likely to say exactly what you wish. This will place you at a disadvantage. Take my advice. Go home again to-day and come next Saturday.

In the meantime you can draw out an additional account, beginning from the date of the mortgage. You whispered to me just now that in point of fact the account just shown me does not contain several of your receipts, as you forgot (!) to put them in. Now just you put them into this new one. And against them put a few items, such as your own long experience will suggest to you—a new ox, a set of earrings for the baby that was born to the eldest daughter whose wedding was the beginning of the account, and so on."

"Ah, yes, to be sure, I understand." Deviditta unloosed the tight rein which had drawn his pony's head almost back on to the saddle peak all these hours, while the poor beast had stood in torture waiting for its master's pleasure to release it, and gaily mounting rode away.   .

That night a dim oil lamp of earth burned long in Deviditta's back room. The jars of turmeric, salt, dried capsicums, sugar, molasses and assafœtida, the tins of Baku kerosene, the parchment carboys of ghi and linseed oil with which the room was lined, stood silent sentinels around the plotter as he painfully deciphered a tattered secret memorandum which contained the true record of all those productions of Bhola's land which had been artfully kept off the other account. The advice of the crafty scrivener was good. It would not do really to deny that these things had come into the money-lender's hands. The evidence against him would have been too strong, and his credit would have suffered. But now they were all recorded in one book or the other, and the fictitious items to be charged against the illiterate victim could all be supported by sworn testimony of some of the twenty craven clients who would not dare to displease the money-lender. The judge would admire his honesty in having recorded every item of receipt, and judgment would surely follow in his favour. Armed with both books, the banking-grocer arrived on the following Saturday. The petition for Rs. 2,115 was soon engrossed upon the requisite stamp, and, accompanied by true copies of the accounts, was handed in to Court, and summons issued to the debtor. True copies of false books or false copies of true books, what matters it? True copies of true books do not pay. False copies of false books are risky and apt to cause explosions when the judge is a vigorous young Englishman. But now all contingencies are guarded against, success is a matter of time only.

The summons was served. Bholā Singh had expected it sooner, and on the day appointed trudged his weary way the whole twenty miles to the Court, having no longer a pony to ride. Patiently he waited till the shadows grew long. He hungrily peered into the open door of the Court and saw the said young Englishman busy writing. "He looks kind and intelligent," thought Bholā Singh. "He is sure to do justice. It still wants an hour of closing time." The hour passed, and yet another. A red-coated peon shouted that no more work could be taken that day, and all cases not heard must stand over till that day fortnight. Devidittā was wreathed in smiles. It was no disappointment to him. He had presented a young heifer to the Court official for the very purpose of securing as many delays in the hearing of the case as possible, that his unyielding debtor should have his twice twenty miles to walk, not once nor twice, but eight or ten times. So it came about that on one pretence or other the mileage traversed by the unhappy old man grew to 320 ere the case finally came on for trial.

"The books are carefully kept, my Lord," whispered the Court official.

"Yes, but I don't like the look of the case," replied the judge. "I think we must try to induce the parties to refer the case to arbitration."

"Oh, no, your Presence," cried Bholā Singh. "Pray

decide it yourself. I cannot afford arbitration. Your Presence does not take bribes."

The Presence kindly observed that this was true, and yet it was true that he had himself not lived in the village these five years and could not possibly tell the rates at which corn, vetches, millet, sugar-cane juice, cotton, and so on had been selling during those years, or whether the articles entered in the second account and denied by the defendant had been really supplied to him or not. Arbitrators would probably be able to make a satisfactory compromise. But Bholā Singh would not listen to any proposal which he well knew meant deeper destitution for him than any blunder which the well-meaning young Englishman could make, though that might be serious enough. The wearied officer at length floundered through the two accounts, and striking out some items which had been insufficiently sustained even by the perjured evidence produced, and also much compound interest, arrived at a decision that Rs. 1,258 were due on the two accounts taken together, and decreed that sum. Both parties instantly announced an intention to appeal. The shades of night were falling. Soon the Court precincts were still, and scores of aching hearts had quitted the scene.

That night was spent by our friend in the city. The next day saw the combatants back at Maure. In the stillness of the twilight of the third day an oily voice sounded at the door of the poverty-stricken courtyard of Bholā Singh. He recognized it as the voice of his rival and cousin Jīwan Singh, to outshine whom had been the bait dangled before his eyes five years before by Devidittā, when the girls' marriages were first discussed. At that time Jīwan Singh had been hated. "Now," said Bholā Singh to himself, "at any rate he is a brother of the same clan. Better than that hateful Khatrī, who knows no ruth nor honour. Jīwan Singh is a Sikh, a khālsā, a true one. Let him in."

He came as an emissary from Deviditta. Kishen Dei sat silently by with a countenance of utter desolation. Her sinking heart was not greatly sustained by the offer which the emissary was empowered to lay before the family. It was this. That if fields numbered 65, 66, 67, 189 were sold outright, the remaining lands, which were half of No. 245, and a fourth share of No. 263, would be released, and Bhola Singh might re-enter upon them.

"I could not do it, Jiwan Singh," was the reply of old Bhola. "You know that, whatever you may be, your son, Jawindh Singh, will succeed you some day. He will be the half-sharer in No. 245, and three-fourths sharer in the other, and he and my descendants are at bitter enmity. It is all we seniors have been able to do to keep them from taking each other's life any time these past ten years, as you know."

"Well, then, what do you say to this? Let the decree holder have his four fields as he wishes. Let me have the whole of No. 263, and you shall have the whole of No. 245 as an exchange, and we shall all live at peace."

This was finally agreed on. Bhola Singh, a few days after, found himself once more full proprietor and in actual possession of six and a half acres of land instead of his original 67 acres odd, and walked a prouder and a happier man in consequence, while the money-lender was owner of five-sixths of the rest, and the ancient rival and enemy owned the remaining one-sixth. It mattered little that the money-lender had all the irrigated and valuable land, that Jiwan Singh had a right of pasture attached to his plot which Bhola Singh had no longer attached to his. The status of an unencumbered landowner had returned to the home. If the valiant Gulab Singh should return from the city of Africa, and the budding young clerk Khazan Singh should rise in the Government service, it might be possible some day to buy other plots, to become prosperous once more. Khazan Singh might even

become a money-lender himself, for had he not learning?
Did he not know English? Was he not a friend of the
magistrate? To be sure this is pretence, but is not life
chiefly pretence? Nay—is it not all māyā (illusion)? Do not
the Shāsters teach us so? What will the next chapter dis-
close? Perhaps the truth! Who knows?

CHAPTER XVII

THAT Devidittā should win was a foregone conclusion, yet the winner was as keen over success and the loser as really overwhelmed in despair as if the chances had been equal on both sides. Bholā Singh relapsed into opium, and Kishen Dei into hard work. The only brightness in her dark sky was the hope of Khazān Singh's promotion and of Gulāb Singh's return. She had had a letter from the latter saying that he was coming home. Nihāl Singh, dimly conscious that he had lost something out of his life now that Bhāg Dei had gone, and wholly conscious of ruin now that they owned but a little land and no oxen, trudged forth daily to the one field. Toil was more than ever necessary. Khazān Singh, now in Government employment, worked with renewed vigour, not as the others, to drown sorrow, but that some day he might avenge the wrong.

Chandkor was cut to the heart. She had felt the loss of her brother much, because she had loved him best ; the death of Bhāg Dei grieved her, because she was the one friend in Maure who had been faithful to her ; but the tale of her father's treachery brought more pain than either.

Miss Gray happened to call upon her at the time, and finding her so sad and down-hearted, stayed with her for a night. This was a pleasure that she had had more than once before.

" I wish I could go home once more."

Miss Gray was surprised.

"Surely you would not risk such a thing! and besides——"

"I know what you mean," interrupted Chandkor, "they don't want to see me. That is the bitterness of it all. Oh! it is hard to go and not be missed, even when one gets love elsewhere."

"Yes, dear, but remember one is sometimes left without the love elsewhere."

"Indeed, I am thankful for it; but my heart is sad!— never to have known a father's or a mother's love, and when a brother—a dear brother—dies, not to be with him, and to feel, as I do now, that the gulf is ever widening, do you think the Lord *can* bridge it over? Do you think all this sin can be forgiven? I do! and I must go to see them and beg of them——"

"Would it be a relief to your mind to see your people . . . even should they not listen to you?"

Chandkor's sad face brightened.

"Ah! yes! even should I fail to see my father I would seek out Gopāl Chand and try to warn him against this . . . treachery . . . which brings body and soul into hell" —she shuddered.

Miss Gray felt anxious. It seemed a risk, even should they go together, and it would in all probability do no good.

Prabhū Dās was at first opposed to the plan, but seeing how his wife suffered, he yielded.

"I need not tell you to take care of her," he said to Miss Gray when they left the next day. Their plan was to stay for the night at the village Mission House and go on to Maure the following day.

Chandkor was very silent—she had had a fearful dream, she said.

The time seemed to pass very slowly, but the day dawned at last, and Miss Gray and her friend went each in her separate doolie across the fields.

When the white tower of Deviditta's house came in sight Chandkor heaved a sigh of relief.

"My dream has not come true after all," she said.

They saw several people standing about, but they were engrossed apparently, and took little notice of them—a circumstance to be thankful for.

"What is that?"

Chandkor grasped Miss Gray's arm and grew white with terror.

It was the sound of mourning.

"Courage ; it may be in another house. Come, dear." And they went swiftly on to Chandkor's old home.

The door stood wide open.

In the courtyard by the fatal well sat Gur Dei, swaying herself to and fro. On a bed lay a still figure covered with a cloth ; sitting near it was Deviditta, not weeping, but looking on his dead with an awful smile.

"Ah ! my pretty maid ! come and look at this !" he cried, as Miss Gray and Chandkor appeared. "It is my son ! Lazy fellow ! I do all the work while he sleeps. Like the other one down the well ! "

Gur Dei looked up. The sight of Chandkor dried her tears.

"How dare you come ! You who have brought the curse upon us. One son drowned, another poisoned, and their father mad ! All because of you ! "

A torrent of abuse poured from her mouth, but Chandkor did not seem to hear. Going up to her father, she knelt down, and laid her strong, soft hands upon him with a tenderness that she had not hitherto dared to show.

"Father, have you gone quite away? Do you not see Chandkor?"

"Chandkor, who ran away ! Ah, yes ! I remember ! Yes ! yes ! but you must look at this lazy one."

Deviditta lifted the chadar from off the face, and patted the cheek with a delighted laugh.

" He won't wake up ! No ! no ! All sleep and no work, while his old father toils alone."

*　　*　　*　　*　　*　　*

Khazan Singh might work on with no thought of revenge. It was done. A mighty hand had fallen, and with a touch had changed Deviditta into another man. The spirit of cunning and grasping had gone, and a spendthrift childishness ruled him instead.

He would go amongst the children of the village trying to play their games, which, as a matter of fact, consisted in a new game of his own : throwing money over their heads, he shouted with glee while they scrambled for the coins.

But his greatest pleasure was to sit by the well, and throw rupees down, one by one. He would listen with his head on one side, like a knowing bird, till the faint splash reached him from the distant water. Then he would smile well content and say :

" Now he has got it ! "

Gur Dei hid all the money away, but somehow he always succeeded in finding it, even as he had succeeded in all things in the past.

Bhola Singh saw him one day at his usual place dropping coins into the well, and his kindly heart forgot its bitterness— forgot even that the silver so recklessly squandered had been gained from him—in its pity for him.

" There is a still deeper depth than poverty," he thought.

CHAPTER XVIII

BHOLĀ SINGH stood under the old banyan tree by one of the many wells without the village, and looked over the fields he had lost, as they lay green and quiet under the level light of evening. A red stain of light from the setting sun fell on the trunk just above his head, flickered and faded, then all the wide land grew purple, as it waited for the night.

The blue smoke rose from the village and a few lamps twinkled like stars on a tomb and on the mosque, for it was Thursday evening, the beginning of Friday, the Sabbath of the Muhamadan Calendar, reckoned by Oriental computation.

Kishen Dei had been out too, and was now returning home. She stopped for a moment by the tree.

"Are you going to stay here all night?" she said. Her face was hard, and her tone harsh. If Bholā Singh had not been just his own simple self, he would have resented it.

"No," he said meekly. "Let us go home."

Kishen Dei walked on in silence, then suddenly stopped and looked eagerly over the fields.

"What is it?" said Bholā Singh stupidly.

"Hush!" she cried, her eyes straining towards a distant figure across the plain.

"Yes, it is he! It is my son!"

They both went to meet him, but Kishen Dei left her husband far behind. Her feet, swift and young again with the strength of love, trod down the cotton and red pepper plants heedless of injury, and soon she was in the arms of her son.

The tall soldier was not ashamed to show his affection, and the heart of his mother was glad.

His father felt a new source of strength in his presence. To his mother he brought rest. Her face grew soft and her voice tender as she looked on his face.

"All will be right now that you have come back," she said.

"All right," echoed Bholā Singh.

And as they walked home together in the gloaming, all crooked things seemed straight, for to the "old folks at home" had arisen light at eventide.

Butler & Tanner, The Selwood Printing Works, Frome, and London.

A NEW BOOK ON INDIA.

Behind the Pardah.

The Story of C.E.Z.M.S. Work in India, by
IRENE H. BARNES
(Authoress of "Behind the Great Wall").

With Illustrations by
PERCY R. CRAFT and JOHN D. MACKENZIE (of Newlyn).

In attractive and durable Cloth Binding, profusely illustrated with
Sixty-eight Beautiful Drawings from Photos lent by
Missionaries from India.

Crown 8vo. Price 3s. 6d.

CONTENTS. — A Glance at the Land. — Behind the Pardah. — Indian Girlhood: Its Ways and Woes. — First Experiences. — Villages and their Visitors. — Indian Women their own Evangelists. — India's Girls for Christ ! — Work for Widows. — Our Suffering Sisters. — The Daughters of Islam.

Forty-five C.E.Z.M.S. Missionaries in India have contributed information for the pages of "BEHIND THE PARDAH."

"**BEHIND THE PARDAH**" is written in a popular style, and will be found acceptable for reading aloud at Missionary Working Parties, as each chapter is a **Complete Story in Itself.** As a Book of Reference it should be in every Reference Library.

N.B.—An Appendix of 30 pages has been prepared for the special use of C.E.Z.M.S. Workers as a Manual of Reference, giving a consecutive outline sketch of the history of the Society from 1880 to 1897, noting all important events connected with the C.E.Z.M.S. in India, from the sailing of its first missionary to the Dismissal Meeting of 1897, and showing the growth of each separate Mission Station. An Alphabetical Index is designed to aid workers suddenly called upon to give Missionary Addresses.

LONDON :
MARSHALL BROTHERS,
KESWICK HOUSE, PATERNOSTER ROW, E.C.
C.E.Z.M.S. : 9, SALISBURY SQUARE, E.C.

www.ingramcontent.com/pod-product-compliance
Lightning Source LLC
Chambersburg PA
CBHW022139020726
47496CB00008B/2473